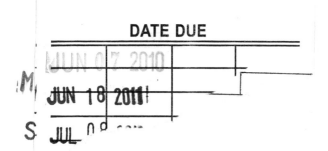

ANIMORPHS ®

The Secret

K.A. Applegate

AN
APPLE
PAPERBACK

SCHOLASTIC INC.
New York Toronto London Auckland Sydney

Cover illustration by Damon C. Torres/The I-Way Company

ISBN 0-590-99729-7

12 11 10 9   9/9 0 1/0

Printed in the U.S.A.

First Scholastic printing, August 1997

For Alexander and Maxx Leach
And always, for Michael

The Secret

CHAPTER 1

My name is Cassie.

I can't tell you my last name. I wish I could. It's kind of a nice last name.

And I can't tell you where I live or the true names of my friends. Why? Because the enemy never stops looking for us.

The enemy. The Yeerks. They're everywhere.

The Yeerks: a parasitic species from a far-distant planet. All they are is little gray slugs, really. I've seen them in their natural state. They look like big snails without the shell. You could squash one under your foot and it would be helpless to stop you.

But the Yeerks don't live out their lives as slugs. Like I said, they are parasites. See, they

1

enter the head of another species, flatten themselves out, and wrap themselves around the brain. And then they take control.

That's what we call a Controller. A human who isn't exactly human anymore. Or a member of any species that is controlled by the Yeerk in its head.

Maybe you think what I've just told you sounds crazy. I guess if I were you, I'd think it was pretty insane. But sometimes even the craziest things happen to be true.

The Yeerks are here. Everywhere. If you think you don't know someone who is a Controller, you're probably wrong.

The school bus driver, the police officer in the patrol car, the minister in the pulpit, the newsman on TV, the rock star in the music video, the person who smiles at you when you ride by on your bike — any one of them might be a Controller. Your teacher, your friend, your sister, your mother and father. Any of them. All of them. And you'll never know. Until it's too late.

Until it is too late for planet Earth.

We fight them. But we're just a handful of kids — Jake, Rachel, Marco, Tobias, Ax, and me. We have some special powers, but we know we can't win this alone. We fight in the hope that someday — someday soon — the Andalites will return and help us.

It was an Andalite prince named Elfangor who

gave us our powers. He was dying. He was desperate. He wanted to do something to help doomed humanity.

He gave us the power to morph. To absorb the DNA of any animal we could touch. To *become* that animal.

So we fight the Yeerks and all their Controllers. The human-Controllers who may once have been our friends and relations. The evil, cannibalistic Taxxon-Controllers, those huge centipedes with their open, gnashing mouths and foul smell. And the deadly, dangerous, but formerly good creatures called Hork-Bajir — the enslaved foot soldiers of the Yeerk empire.

And we fight Visser Three. Leader of the Yeerk invasion of Earth. The only Andalite-Controller in existence. The only Yeerk who, like us, has the power to morph.

The murderer of Elfangor. A killer. A destroyer. The creature who would make slaves of all humans and destroy our planet.

Unless someone stops him. Unless we stop him.

Five ordinary kids and a young Andalite we call Ax, against all the might of the Yeerk empire.

We call ourselves Animorphs.

We're only supposed to use our power for fighting the Yeerks. But there are times when it comes in handy for other things.

My best friend Rachel and I were at school, in the dark and gloomy science lab. The final bell had rung and kids were tearing out of there at top speed, running for the buses or their parents' cars.

You know how it is — when the school day is over you just want *out* of there. But I had been messing up in school lately. See, I have kind of a busy life. My dad runs the Wildlife Rehabilitation Clinic in our barn. I help out there, taking care of injured or sick animals. Plus the whole Animorph thing takes up a lot of time.

Anyway, I had to do a makeup project for science class. I built a maze for a rat I'd named Courtney. I mean, I figured an animal project would be easy for me. I've *been* more animals than a lot of kids have seen.

Courtney was supposed to find her way through the cardboard maze to the end, where I had placed some tasty seeds and nuts. Then I would make notes on her progress. How hard could that be?

Rachel stared at me. She tapped her foot impatiently. She looked down at her watch. Then she looked up at the clock on the wall. "You know, school's been out for ten minutes, and here I am, still at school. This can't be right. It's unnatural."

4

"Why can't she figure out the maze?" I wondered out loud. "What's the problem?"

"A stupid rat? Er, I mean, maybe you have a not very smart rat. That could be the subject of your paper — 'My Dumb Rat.'"

"What is the problem with you?" I demanded, ignoring Rachel and talking directly to the rat. I took Courtney from her cage and stuck her in the high-walled maze. "Smell the nuts. Smell the nuts and then find your way through the maze."

Courtney looked up at me and twitched her nose.

"That's not an answer," I said. "I *need* this grade. I am not going to try and explain a *D* to my parents just because you can't get it together."

"A *D*!" Rachel echoed. "You're looking at a *D*? No way."

"Rachel, why do you think I'm here? Because I'm trying to go from an *A* to an *A+*? Yes. I am looking at a *D*. And I can't bring my parents a *D*. That would mean weeks of them going, 'Where did we go wrong? We must be failing as parents. We have to spend more time with Cassie, helping her every night with her homework.'"

Rachel shuddered at the absolute horror of that scenario.

"Hey," Rachel said. "Morph the rat. Maybe you can see what his . . . her . . . its problem is."

"I could do that," I said slowly. "But see, if Jake found out . . . You know the rule: No morphing except when necessary."

Rachel shrugged. "It's necessary that I get out of here. It's necessary that you don't get a bad grade. Look at that — two necessities at once!"

I probably shouldn't have let her talk me into it. Except, actually, I'd already been considering it. That's the great thing about Rachel — she's always willing to help talk you into doing something you probably shouldn't do.

"You have to do it, too," I said.

"Why? Why do I have to morph a rat?"

"Remember the time you wanted to scare that guy with the elephants? Wasn't I there for you then? Besides, we can't leave till I try to figure this out."

Rachel rolled her eyes. "Ooookay. That made absolutely *no* sense, but I'll do it anyway. Let's just get it over with."

Acquiring an animal's DNA isn't very complicated. All you do is touch it, and focus your mind on the animal. The animal gets kind of sleepy, kind of dopey. In a minute it's all over, and a new DNA pattern is swimming around inside you.

"I have the feeling this is a stupid idea," Rachel said.

I was piling up books to make steps so we

could climb into the maze once we morphed. "Well, it was your idea, Rachel."

"Oh, yeah. My idea. Like I'm the one who cares how the rat handles a maze. Let's get this over with before someone decides to check in on us," she said. Already, she was beginning to change.

I focused my thoughts, forming a mental picture of the rat. And then . . . I felt the change begin.

I was shrinking. Shrinking very fast. For a human, I'm not very big. In fact, I'm kind of short. But I was a lot bigger than a rat, so it was a pretty big change in size.

My T-shirt and my jeans were suddenly very loose.

I looked at Rachel. Huge long whiskers were growing out of her still-human mouth.

The side of the cabinets beside me grew higher and higher. They had originally been maybe three feet high. Soon they seemed as tall as a three-story building. The grain in the wood looked like huge swirling patterns, like strange paintings the size of murals.

The one-foot squares of tan and green linoleum seemed to double and triple and quadruple in size, until each was as big as a parking space.

As I shrank, my clothes folded and billowed down over me like a collapsed circus tent.

My skin turned a sort of pinkish-gray, then suddenly sprouted white fur. My legs were shriveling. My arms were shriveling. My face bulged like a zit about to pop. My nose poked way out, farther and farther. My face became pointed.

And then, the rat's senses replaced my own.

On came the ears, like someone had thrown a switch. On came the nose.

And on came the rat's instincts, bubbling up in my human mind and carrying their messages of fear and hunger and more fear.

<Yikes!> Rachel commented. <Nervous little things, aren't they?>

CHAPTER 2

The rat's eyes weren't any better than my own. In fact, they weren't quite as good. Like lots of animals I've been, the eyes were better at seeing movement than at seeing colors and shapes. Nothing was moving, so my vision was kind of, I don't know . . . kind of dull.

I could see Rachel well enough, though. We were made from the same rat's DNA, so were basically the same rat. I could see her long, naked pink tail. That tail is the reason people hate rats, but think squirrels are cute.

That, plus the fact that rats have been known to nibble on humans from time to time.

The rat's hearing was excellent, but it was its sense of smell that was really amazing. I

9

twitched my little rat nose and the whole world sent me messages.

I smelled the chemicals in the cabinets. I smelled the lingering aromas of hundreds of different kids who had passed through the room that day. I even smelled the seeds and nuts in the maze, up on the table.

I felt the rat's brain beginning to surge more strongly up beneath my own. The rat instincts were coming out. Fear. Not the sharp sudden fear a human might feel. It was the eternal fear of a small animal in a world of great big predators.

And the hunger. The hunger of a tiny animal who will spend its entire life, every single minute of its life, searching for its next meal.

But there was also the intelligence.

When you morph an animal, its instincts come through. You don't get its memories, usually, but you do get its instincts. Its basic abilities are there.

This rat was very nervous. It was afraid of being out in the open. It wanted to be next to the wall so that enemies would have a harder time attacking it. I decided that wasn't a bad instinct.

<Maybe we should get somewhere safer?> I asked Rachel in thought-speak.

<Oh, yes, definitely,> she agreed.

The little rat legs powered up and we took off.

10

Not fast, really, but it seemed fast because I was so low to the ground. My nose was just a quarter of an inch above the linoleum. As I waddle-walked along I saw huge walls looming over me — the sides of the lab tables. And I saw sparse forests of trees — actually the legs of chairs.

I scooted along the corner of the wall with Rachel right behind me.

<That is not an attractive tail,> Rachel said. <I mean, I'm a rat and I still think it looks bad.>

Then I saw the table where my maze was set up. The real Courtney was up there. I checked out the area.

<I think we can climb up my backpack onto the chair. Then onto my sweater, then jump to the tabletop.>

<I'm following you,> Rachel said. <Lead the way, Rat-girl.>

The rat body was amazingly good at climbing and scampering up to the tabletop. You wouldn't think that squat body and those stubby little legs would be good for climbing, but I really do believe that rat could have gone just about anywhere it wanted to go.

I saw the pile of books I'd left as a sort of stairway up the outer wall of the maze. And now that I was rat-sized, that wall really was a wall. It looked about nine feet high.

<You go do the maze,> Rachel said. <I'll wait out here.>

I scampered quickly up over the books. The pictures on the front of my science book looked like huge mosaics made of colored tiles.

I reached the top and gazed down into the maze. I knew I could jump down in there, down into those long hallways, but at that moment I was afraid. It was odd, but the idea of running into the real Courtney made me nervous. I've always felt a little funny about using animals' bodies. It makes me feel a little guilty somehow.

But I had a job to do. I had to figure out why Courtney couldn't find the nuts. She should be able to smell them . . .

<Hey. Wait a minute. I can't smell them, either. Not at all.>

<Can't smell what?> Rachel asked.

<The nuts. I can't smell them.>

<Do I care?>

<It's the whole point,> I said.

I looked around, puzzled. Then I noticed the breeze. I aimed my rat eyes upward. There, a million miles up, as far away as the moon, was a ceiling fan.

If I'd had lips, I would have smiled.

<Hey. It's the fan. It's blowing the scent of the nuts away.>

<Great. Now can we get out of here?>

I was feeling pretty satisfied with my insight when two things happened at once. First, Courtney — the real Courtney — came zooming around the corner of the maze.

The second thing was that I heard a loud crash, a roar of loud laughter, and the rushing approach of footsteps.

Courtney froze and stared at me. I stared at her. Then I looked back at Rachel. Rachel was frozen, same as me.

"HEY, LOOK! RATS!" an impossibly loud voice shouted. A boy, I was sure of that. I didn't recognize the specific voice, but I recognized the tone. He was looking for trouble.

"GROSS!" another voice shouted. "SOMEONE SHOULD EXTERMINATE 'EM. I HATE RATS!"

Two of them. Two guys playing around. Two jerks looking for something to break or destroy.

Two very, very big creatures compared to us tiny rats.

Sudden shadows! Vibrations. Huge movements!

WHAM!

The table shook like it was hit by a massive earthquake!

WHAM! THUD!

A shadow, moving fast, descending on me. I jumped!

THUD!

The tabletop jumped from the impact of the boy's hand slamming down near me.

I felt the maze being lifted. It tilted wildly up on its side. I could see the entire maze, now a wall instead of a floor.

Courtney fell out of the maze onto the table. Now there were three of us, trapped on the table-top.

"HERE! A BROOM!"

<Bail!> Rachel yelled.

<Run!> I cried.

THWACK!

Something the size of a pine tree slapped the surface of the table. It was a broom handle. The handle swept across the table, coming right at us, a wooden log half my own height.

I jumped. Rats don't look like jumpers, but when they have to, they can.

Up! Over the broom handle, Rachel right beside me. I saw Courtney haul in the other direction.

Run! Run! Run! Rachel and I moved out at top rat speed.

The edge of the table!

It was like standing on the edge of a four-story building. It looked like a very, very long way down.

Then, a shadow! A disturbance in the airflow! No time to look! No time to think!

<Aaaaahhhh!>

<Aaaaahhhh!>

We leaped from the edge of the table just as the broom handle slammed down in the very spot where we'd been standing.

The fall seemed to take forever. It was like skydiving. The linoleum tiles looked like some strange farmlands far beneath me.

I hit the floor hard. My legs didn't catch the impact. They were too short. My big furry belly took the blow. But it knocked the wind out of me.

As my mind cleared, I realized the guys were no longer after me and Rachel. They had Courtney in a corner. They were jabbing at her with the broom handle.

<Oh, man,> I said. <If we survive, Jake is going to kill me for this.>

<I'm tired of running,> Rachel said. <Let's kick some butt.>

That, of course, is classic Rachel. We were each about a foot long, counting our tail. So naturally, she thought we should attack some guys the size of Godzilla.

But you know what? I was tired of running, too. And I couldn't let poor Courtney get killed. She was more than just a science project. Now she was sort of a sister rat.

I aimed right for the leg of the nearest guy. It was the size of a redwood, except that this redwood was blue. Baggy blue denim.

15

<Are you thinking what I'm thinking?> I asked Rachel.

<I'm with you,> she said.

We motored our tiny rat feet and shot forward. Faster, faster, as fast as we could go. Which, happily, turned out to be fairly fast.

Up the pants leg! I saw a flash of skin above the socks. I went for it. My tiny clawed feet grabbed onto that white gym sock and went straight up.

It was like going into a tunnel. The rough denim of the jeans scraped along my head and back. The pink flesh curved away beneath me. I dug my claws, front and back, into the skin and hairs of that huge leg, and shot wildly up the back of his leg.

"AAAAAAHHHHHH!"

Suddenly, the boy was no longer interested in Courtney.

"AAAAAAHHHHHH! IT'S ON ME! IT'S ON ME! GET IT OFF! GET IT OFF MEEEEE!"

"NOOOO! OH! OH! OH!" the other boy screamed, as Rachel attacked.

<Yaaahhhh!> I cried, as the leg was thrown wildly back and forth. I slammed against the denim wall. I was slammed back against the curved pink skin. I scrambled wildly to hold on as the boy screamed and ran and shook his leg like a lunatic.

"AAAAAHHH! AAAAAAHHH! AAAAAHHHH!"

Out of the science lab we tore. Out into the hallway, with the two guys screaming the whole way.

I turned myself around, with great difficulty, and aimed downward. Out I shot. Out of the pants leg to freedom.

The last I saw of the two guys, they were still running in sheer panic.

I never did see Courtney again. I guess she found a place to live in the school walls. At least I'd figured out why she wouldn't go through the maze.

Rachel and I found a safe place to demorph. Then we went to her house and gave her little sister a home perm. Business as usual.

CHAPTER 3

That evening, everyone came over. We usually hook up at the Wildlife Rehabilitation Clinic. Also known as my barn.

I guess we all get together once or twice a week. More often when there's a "mission" of some kind. I was surprised when Jake called to say we should get together because it had only been a couple of days since the last meeting. And as far as I knew, nothing serious had been planned.

I hoped this was *only* a meeting and nothing else. I had like zero spare time. School. Life. That stuff takes time, you know?

I was cleaning the cages when the others started to arrive. It was a raccoon cage, to be specific. This raccoon had been hit a glancing blow by a car on the highway. A lot of the highway patrol guys know to call us if they see an injured animal by the road.

The raccoon would be okay, thanks to my dad. But in the meantime, it had to be fed and watered and medicated and its cage had to be kept clean. And all of that was my job.

I was wearing dirty overalls and big tall rubber boots. My arms were deep inside rubber gloves when Rachel showed up.

"Hey, Cassie."

"Hi, Rachel." I was bent over, concentrating on wiping out the raccoon's cage. I could tell the raccoon was seriously considering leaping on my face and chewing my nose.

"So. Cassie. You get that outfit at Banana Republic? Or is that the new Express line?"

Rachel and I are best friends, but we are very different people. If you just saw Rachel walking by you'd probably think typical airhead mallcrawler. If you took a closer look you'd start to think, *No, she's actually very beautiful, not typical at all.*

And if you took a third look, she'd probably come over, get in your face, and say, "What are you staring at? Hello? You have some kind of a problem?"

Rachel is tall and blond and beautiful and

fearless. She's *Xena: Warrior Princess* — only without the leather.

We must be the most mismatched best friends in history. Rachel could walk through the mosh pit at Lollapalooza on a rainy day and come out the other side looking like one of those models in *Glamour*. I, on the other hand, will show up for my own wedding someday dressed in jeans and boots and socks that don't match.

I stood back from the raccoon cage. I smiled and gave a little twirl so Rachel could admire the outfit. "You like it? It's part of the Ralph Lauren Animal Poop collection."

"Someday I am going to knock you over the head, stuff you in a big bag, drag you to the mall, and force you to buy a dress. You can keep the big rubber boots, if you insist, but we're getting you a dress."

"You're kidding, right?" I asked Rachel. You can never be totally sure with Rachel.

She just smiled with her ten thousand bright white teeth.

I heard the sound of bikes being leaned up against the outside of the barn. Then I heard male voices.

"Batman could beat Spiderman? You expect me to take that seriously? Are you insane? I thought I knew you, Jake, but you're obviously an

20

idiot. No offense. Spiderman would annihilate Batman."

Marco. Marco, sounding as serious as Marco is capable of sounding.

"Two words: body armor. Spiderman's webs would not stick to Batman's body armor. Homer, stay out here, boy. You can't go in."

That would be Jake. And Homer, his dog. Homer is not allowed in the barn. Being a dog, Homer believes small animals are meant to be chased.

Jake and Marco came through the small side door of the barn. Jake was in the lead, as usual. If we Animorphs have a leader, it's Jake. He's strong, inside and out. And really good-looking. Also inside and out. I mean, he's just an amazingly cool guy.

Jake has had to grow up a lot in a very short time. It's weird to be a kid, and yet act like some kind of a general or something. We all decide the big stuff together. But when we're in a fight, it's Jake who has to make the little decisions a lot of times. The little decisions that could leave one of his friends dead.

It made me smile to realize that Jake could still enjoy absurd arguments with Marco. I sort of worry about the pressure on Jake.

Jake and I are kind of . . . you know. We like each other. As in *like*.

21

Marco was just behind Jake. He's smaller than Jake, with longer, darker hair, laughing, dark eyes, and an attitude.

Marco thinks the whole world is just a setup for a joke. Marco will tell a joke while he's bleeding and terrified and in pain. But there are times when his eyes lose their skeptical expression and grow glittery and dangerous.

"Cassie," Marco said, "you look beautiful, as always. Your use of manure as a fashion statement is so tasteful." Then he gazed at Rachel and winced. "Yikes! Everytime I see you, you're taller. Stop it. Stop growing."

Rachel patted Marco on his head. "Don't worry. I don't look down on you for being short, Marco. I look down on you just for being you."

Marco grabbed his chest in pain. "Aargh! And Xena puts another spear in me."

"Hi, Jake," I said, ignoring the usual Marco-versus-Rachel stuff.

"Hi, Cassie," he said. He gave me one of his rare, slow smiles. "Hey, I heard this weird story. These two guys at school claim they were attacked by a pair of lab rats."

"Really? I didn't hear about that," I said, trying not to make the fakey, shrill sound I always make when I'm lying.

Jake raised one eyebrow and I quickly went back to cleaning out the cage.

"What are we here for?" Rachel asked bluntly.

Jake shrugged. "Tobias told me to get everyone together. He and Ax have something."

Right on cue, we heard a flutter of wings. A hawk shot in through the open hayloft above. It turned sharply, killed its speed, swept its talons forward, and landed neatly on a rafter.

It was a red-tailed hawk. Mostly brown on its back, a lighter, mottled brown and tan beneath. The bird took its name from its tail feathers, which were the color of rust.

The hawk glared down at us with unbelievably intense brown and gold eyes.

<Hi,> the hawk said, a silent voice that we heard only in our heads.

"Hi, Tobias," I answered.

Tobias is the fifth human member of our group. Although he's not entirely human anymore. See, if you stay more than two hours in a morph, you stay forever.

In his mind and heart, Tobias is still a human being — mostly. But he has the body of a hawk. He lives as a hawk.

"Hi, Tobias," Rachel said. "I thought maybe you'd stop by last night."

Tobias sometimes hangs out with Rachel. He flies into her upstairs room and watches TV, or reads. Things he can't do in the wild. Human things.

<Um, well, I was going to,> he said in thought-speak. <But there was this thing with Ax . . . >

Ax is Aximili-Esgarrouth-Isthill. He's the sixth person in our group. He's even less human than Tobias. Ax is an Andalite.

"Speaking of which, is Ax coming?" Jake asked.

<No. He's still out keeping an eye on things. Or four eyes, actually.>

"What things?" Marco asked, beginning to sound impatient.

Tobias swooped down to be closer. He landed on the top edge of a stall door. He checked out the many cages. At the moment we had, in addition to the raccoon, a fox, two wolves, a handful of various bats, a really cool porcupine, a pair of jackrabbits, a deer that had been mauled by a bear, several doves, a goose, a swan cygnet, a whole group of assorted gulls, a beautiful red-winged blackbird, and a barn owl.

<What happened to the golden eagle?> Tobias asked.

"He's all better so we released him," I admitted. See, golden eagles occasionally kill and eat hawks. "We released him way back in the hills, though. Nowhere near your territory, Tobias."

Tobias didn't look too happy. But then, Tobias has a hawk's face, so he never looks anything but fierce. Once he was a very sweet, slightly dopey kid. Jake and he met when Jake stopped some bullies from sticking Tobias's head in the toilet.

<Anyway. I have something to report. It looks like someone is getting ready to start logging in the forest.>

"No way!" I cried.

The others were less upset.

"So what?" Marco asked.

"So habitat will be destroyed! So animals will be made homeless! So old-growth trees will be chopped down to make plywood!" I cried. "That's so what."

Marco frowned. "And I care about this . . . why?"

I started to answer, but Tobias cut me off. <You don't care, Marco. But you might care about *who* is doing the logging.>

"I'm guessing a logging company," Marco suggested.

<Yeah. You're right,> Tobias said. <Only this logging company has built a command center deep in the forest. A log building, actually, like you'd expect. Except for one little thing.>

"What one little thing?" Jake asked.

<The building is protected by a force field. A force field that seems to stop anything that gets near. I tried to fly closer, and it was like hitting a wall. Also, there are armed guards walking the

perimeter around the building, and patrolling up and down the access road.>

"Oh," Jake said.

<Guards armed with automatic rifles.>

"Yeerks?" Rachel wondered. "But why would the Yeerks want to be logging in the forest?"

I knew the answer to that question. The Yeerks' plan was all too obvious. "They want to destroy habitat," I said.

"What? Now the Yeerks are out to destroy the deer and the owls?" Marco said with a dismissive laugh.

"No," I said. "It's not owl habitat they want to destroy. They're after a different species."

<Yeah,> Tobias agreed. <They're going to wipe out the habitat of the very, *very* endangered Animorph.>

CHAPTER 4

"So. The Yeerks are right there in our forest. Fine," Rachel said with her usual enthusiasm for anything dangerous. "Let's go take a look."

"If this is a Yeerk operation, we have to be careful," Marco said. "They're expecting us."

<Expecting us?> Tobias said.

Marco nodded. "Look, the Yeerks believe we're a band of Andalites, right? They think only Andalites can morph. They've figured out that the forest is the only place a group of Andalites could be hiding. Let's face it — if we *were* Andalites, we wouldn't exactly be able to rent an apartment."

"So we'd be in the forest. Just like Ax is right

now." Jake nodded. "They want to use the logging operation as a way to go Andalite-hunting."

"Right. Which means they think we're out in the forest. So they have to be prepared for an attack. They are going to be totally ready for any strange group of animals that show up."

I agreed with Marco. But there was another question that was bothering me. "How did they ever get permission to cut trees in a national forest?"

Marco rolled his eyes, like I was being an idiot. "Who cares? The fact is, they did."

"If we're going to take a look at this place, we can't show up there in a big group," Jake said. "We split up, go in two groups. In different morphs. We see what we see, but we do nothing. Agreed?"

Everyone nodded.

"So. If it's okay with everyone, I'll go in with Rachel. I'll morph the peregrine falcon. Rachel, you can morph your bald eagle. Tobias will show us the way. That's a lot of excellent eyes to look things over. Cassie, you go in with Marco. Get a different perspective."

"Why can't I go with Rachel?" I asked. It's not that I don't like Marco. He just grinds my nerves sometimes.

"Because you and Rachel just egg each other on," Jake said.

He knew about the rat thing. He definitely

28

knew. Still, it kind of bothered me. "Oh, you mean like you and Marco egg each other on?"

Jake nodded and gave me a wink. "You could say that. Yep. Exactly."

Ten minutes later, Marco and I were walking across the far fields of my farm, wading through tall grass toward the edge of the forest.

The forest is huge. It reaches all the way back up into the mountains. Thousands, maybe millions of square miles of pines and oaks and a scattering of birch trees sweep down from the mountains all the way to the edges of town. Our farm is right on the edge. Lots of farms are. And some new housing developments and so on.

It was a clear evening, so the mountains showed up pink and lavender in the setting sun. There was a cool breeze, loaded with the smell of wildflowers. Two of our horses were grazing off across the field by the fence. It was a safe area, so we let the horses run free at night in nice weather.

Of course, now that wolves were being reintroduced into the forest, we might have to change that. A wolf pack can bring down even a healthy, strong horse. I know. I've been a wolf.

And I was getting ready to be one again.

We reached the edge of the forest. It began very suddenly. One step was on grass, the next step was on pine needles and fallen leaves.

It was darker under the trees. And as we walked into the forest it grew darker still. I craned my neck back. Looking up, I could still see blue sky overhead. But the sun was going down, and night was growing near. Creatures of the day were winding down their activities, and creatures of the night were opening their eyes.

"Might as well morph now," Marco said.

"Yes. We'll move faster in wolf morph," I agreed.

He grinned at me. "Does it ever creep you out? All this morphing, I mean? I still remember the first time. It was so bizarre."

"It's still bizarre," I said.

"Even for you?"

"Why not for me?" I asked.

Marco shrugged. "You're the morphing queen."

I laughed. "Oh please. We all morph."

"Yeah, but even Ax says you have some kind of special talent. Like you have more control or whatever. He says you're even better than he is."

"That doesn't make it any less creepy for me," I said. "I mean, we're in the forest, the sun is going down, and I'm getting ready to turn into a wolf. This could be a horror movie."

"*Wolfman.*"

"*Wolfwoman*," I corrected.

"*The Wolf Couple.*"

We shoved our outer clothing under some brush, and I began to morph. I focused my mind on the wolf whose DNA was a part of me. Marco and I were actually the identical wolf. We had both absorbed the DNA of the same female.

I felt my jaw stretching and stretching outward. The bones made a slight grinding sound as my small, weak human mouth became the powerful, crushing jaw of the wolf. My human mouth and teeth could barely cut through a tough steak. The wolf jaw and teeth could tear the throat out of a living, struggling deer.

My gums itched as my teeth grew longer.

"See? Thrat's whuk I mearrrn," Marco said, trying to make sounds even as his human tongue and lips disappeared. In a few more seconds he was able to switch to thought-speak.

<See? That's what I mean. Look at how much better you are at morphing than I am. That looks very creepy, by the way.>

I had controlled the morphing so that the wolf's head appeared completely formed before anything else happened. I was a completely normal girl with just the downiest growth of fur and a massive, shaggy wolf's head atop my shoulders.

<I didn't really think much about it,> I said. <Sometimes my brain just seems to have its own ideas about morphing.>

The rest of the morph continued. My knees reversed direction. My legs grew smaller. Rough pads replaced my feet. The fur on my body grew long and rough and grayish in color.

I fell forward onto my front legs, no longer able to stand.

The wolf's instincts began to surface, but I had done this morph before, so I could handle them easily.

Then the wolf's senses came on, replacing my human perception.

The forest was an entirely different experience to the wolf. It was as if I had been transported instantly to some totally different place.

My human ears had noticed almost nothing — a bit of wind, a few chirps, the rustling of leaves. But the wolf's ears heard everything. They heard some large, four-footed animal about a hundred yards to the right. They heard squirrels gnawing acorns in their high nests. They heard insects crawling beneath the pine-needle floor. They heard cars on the far-distant road.

And the ears were nothing, compared to the sense of smell.

Let me just put it this way — in terms of smell, all humans are blind. We smell nothing. Maybe we smell a flower if it's right under our nose, or a chocolate cake baking in the oven. But we are the morons of smell.

Wolves are the geniuses of smell. You have no idea. No idea at all what it is like to have that wolf nose.

<Ahhh!> I cried in shock.

<Yeah,> Marco agreed. <I'd forgotten. Wow. Hello!>

It is exactly like being blind and then, all of a sudden, being able to see.

The wolf smelled the horses in our field. The wolf didn't just smell that they were horses, it smelled that they were fully grown and healthy. The wolf smelled every flower, every tree, every leaf, every mushroom. It smelled water in three different locations and knew which stream was sweetest.

The wolf smelled a chipmunk, a dozen squirrels, voles, rats, mice, deer, a dead sparrow, a raccoon, no . . . two raccoons.

And it smelled *me.* I mean, it smelled my scent from the clothing I had just morphed out of. It smelled the scent of all the birds and animals in my barn that I had touched or even walked near.

It smelled things that were three days old. The human who had walked through these woods days before. The other wolf, an old male, who had passed by. The smell of dogs and cats and trash.

And one very strange smell that I realized had to be the scent of an Andalite — Ax.

When you put it all together in your head —
the sense of smell and the hearing — it was as if
the entire world around you was crawling and
seething and exploding with life.

<Cool,> Marco said.

<Way cool,> I agreed. <Let's go. Let's run.>

Wolves like to run.

CHAPTER 5

Wolves can run. Wolves can run all through the night, without stopping or slowing or taking a break.

We ran, Marco and I, jumping fallen logs, swerving through trees, and skirting patches of thorns. Across sunset-lit meadows, and through dark stands of tall pines. We splashed happily through streams and skittered across rocks.

We were running on sensation, our heads swimming with smell and sound and sight. There was nothing within a thousand yards that we didn't know about. We were plugged into the data stream of nature itself.

We smelled the logging camp long before we reached it. Then we heard the sounds of ma-

35

chines. And we heard the murmurs of conversation. Human voices.

Then we got a reminder that we were not the only hyper-alert predators in the forest.

<Is that you guys?> a thought-speak voice asked. Jake's voice.

<Yes. Where are you?> I asked.

<Way up above you,> Jake said with a laugh. I stopped running and craned my head back like I was going to howl at the moon. Through a break in the trees I saw a patch of sky. And way, way up in that sky, I saw three tiny black dots.

Tobias and Jake, floating a quarter-mile up. Even in the weakening light they had seen us from clear up in the bellies of the clouds.

<The place is just ahead. Lots of heavy equipment. Guards. But go take a look. Just be careful.>

<We'd hang out, but the sun's going down and we won't be able to see much more anyway,> Tobias remarked.

<You saw us,> I said, a bit grumpily.

Tobias laughed. <Yeah, but you're a pair of great big wolves. That's not much of a challenge. Now, that flea crawling by your ear . . . >

<You can't see a flea,> I said.

<Heh, heh, heh,> Tobias answered. <Can't I?>

Marco and I started moving forward again, but slower than before. More cautiously.

Through the trees we began to see light. Artificial light.

We crept slowly nearer, shoulders hunched, heads low, ears aimed forward, sniffing the wind for clues.

The command center building was bigger than it had looked at first. It was made of logs, like some kind of rustic ranger station. It was two stories tall, with a porch on the front.

On the back-and-side ground levels there were no windows. None at all. There were windows on the upper level, but they were dark. Too dark for me to see into.

There were blindingly bright spotlights mounted atop the building. The forest had been cut back a hundred feet or so on all sides of the building, and the bare, scarred earth all around was lit as bright as the sunniest day.

A dozen or so huge pieces of equipment were parked neatly side by side. Earthmovers, oddly shaped cranes, trucks, and some monstrous thing that looked like a huge kid's toy. I guessed that it was used to cut trees.

My heightened wolf senses noticed several men walking around the perimeter of the clearing. They were spaced about fifty yards apart and seemed very alert.

The nearest one was walking just in front of

us. Marco and I crouched low behind tree trunks and stood perfectly still.

The man wore a tan uniform. The legs of his pants were tucked into high leather boots. He was carrying an automatic rifle.

<Okay, this *does* look just slightly extreme for a logging camp. That guy is no lumberjack,> I said.

I aimed my ears at the building, but no sounds came from inside. Either there was no one in there or they had soundproofed the place really well.

<Are you getting anything?> Marco asked me.

<Not from inside the building. But I'm smelling stuff that I can't recognize. Weird smells.>

<Yeah. Me, too. Animal smells, but weird, you know?>

<Hork-Bajir?>

<Could be,> Marco said.

<The guards are all human,> I pointed out. <You know, this may have nothing to do with the Yeerks. Maybe whoever these guys are, they're up to something totally different. I mean, normal humans do act strange sometimes. Not every weird person is a Controller.>

<No. But don't forget — the force field. Even if these guys were like drug dealers or something, I don't think they'd have a force field.>

<Good point.> I fell silent. I had heard a noise. Several noises. Movement. Careful, stealthy movement.

I glanced at Marco. I saw that his ears were pricked up, too. <Yeah, I heard that,> Marco said. <Behind us. Someone circling around.>

I felt the knife edge of fear. The human part of me was afraid. The wolf me was not. But I trusted the human instinct more on this.

<Where are the guards?> I asked.

<Uh-oh,> Marco said.

Blinding light!

Light everywhere. Everywhere! The whole world was a brilliant white.

I felt like the whole universe could see me.

BLAM! BLAM! BLAM!

The sound of sharp, cracking explosions in the trees above us. I glanced up. Something falling. A net!

Big steel nets were exploding from the trees above us, falling toward us. There were heavy weights at the edges.

<RUN!>

We bolted. The net above me fell. I was racing the falling edge, racing, racing . . .

Free!

The net scraped my back. But I was out from under!

TSEWWW! TSEWWW!

A brilliant stab of red light shot from the dark upper windows of the log building. The beam hit the base of a tree not six inches from me. The wood was vaporized. A six-inch hole was blown right through its trunk.

Dracon beams!

I started to run. But something felt wrong. Marco! Where was he?

I turned and looked back. He was under the net! He was weighed down and crawling on his belly to get free of it.

I ran back.

TSEWWW! TSEWWW!

The Dracon beams, almost pale in the brilliant floodlit woods, fired again and again.

I grabbed the edge of the net in my jaws and lifted it up. It was shockingly heavy. No wonder Marco was crawling.

<Get out of here!> Marco yelled. <Don't get killed for me.>

<Shut up and come on!> I cried.

TSEWWW! TSEWWW!

I couldn't hold the net. My jaws were aching. My neck was dragging down. Marco was barely inching forward. The Dracon beams were getting more and more accurate.

And now I saw where the guards had disappeared to. They were running through the woods toward us. Half a dozen men carrying automatic weapons. It was an eerie and terrifying sight, as the men cast gigantic shadows up into the tree-tops.

Then . . . something fast. Faster than a wolf. Faster than a human.

Like a deer. Like a horse. A mouthless face, eyes on stalks, a tail like a scorpion. A creature like nothing that lived on Earth. It raced straight for us.

<Ax!> I cried.

His tail struck, faster than a human eye could follow.

The tail blade made sparks as it sliced through the net, leaving a long gash just in front of Marco's nose.

<Yikes! That was a little close!> Marco said. But he surged through the hole in the net and took off. I was right behind him. Wolves are already fast. But when you get a scared wolf with a scared human mind inside it, you'd be amazed how that animal can move.

We hauled our butts out of there, with Ax right beside us.

BAMBAMBAMBAMBAMBAMBAMBAM!

Gunfire! Good, old-fashioned, human, very deadly gunfire.

It's much louder in reality than it is in movies.

And it's much scarier to have it aimed at you than it is to see it in a movie. Basically, getting shot at is absolutely *nothing* like a movie.

<Aaaaahhh!> I yelled.

<Aaaaahhh!> Marco yelled.

<Aaaaahhh!> Ax agreed.

Two wolves and an Andalite set a new record speeding away from that place.

CHAPTER 6

"Okay, I think we've answered the question about whether that's just an ordinary logging camp," Marco said.

We had reached the far edge of the forest, back close to my farm. Marco and I had demorphed. Rachel and Jake flew down and joined us. Tobias took up a perch on a low branch.

Ax stood nearby. His two stalk eyes moved continuously, side to side, peering into the dark woods around us. His two main eyes met my gaze.

"By the way, thanks, Ax," I said.

"Yeah, no kidding," Marco added. "I was Spam back there. That tail blade of yours is something."

<I should have spotted the nets up in the treetops,> Ax berated himself. <I had detected the force field and I suspected there were Dracon beams in the upper windows. But the nets were so primitive I overlooked them.>

Ax, like all Andalites, has no spoken speech. Probably because they have no mouths. Thought-speak is his natural language.

Up close he looks like a cross between a deer or a horse, and a human and a scorpion. Sort of like a mythical centaur. His upper body is like a boy's. He has weak-looking arms and a head with two movable stalks on top, kind of like antlers. Each stalk has an eye. The eyes are constantly looking left and right and back.

Andalites are very hard to sneak up on.

His body is covered in blue and tan fur, very short on his humanoid torso, a bit longer on his deerlike body. His four hooves are sharp and black.

But it's the tail that grabs your attention. It's long enough that he can whip it up over his head and hit someone standing in front of him. It ends in a curved blade.

"None of us saw the nets," Jake pointed out. "They must have been well-concealed."

"The point is, they were waiting for us," Marco said. "This is definitely a Yeerk operation. I don't think they really want to go into the lumberjack business, which means this whole thing is about getting us."

"Agreed," Rachel said tersely. "They think we're Andalites. They know we've been hurting them all around this area. They've decided we must be hiding in these woods."

"They're almost right," Jake pointed out. "Ax and Tobias both do live in the forest. And we do use the forest."

"You know, we're not the only thing going on here," I said.

They all looked puzzled.

I took a deep breath. "I mean, you know, this forest is important even if Tobias and Ax weren't here. It makes me sick to think of people chopping down all these trees."

"Oh, puh-leeze, not the Earth-Mother thing, okay?" Marco said. "I almost got myself fried by a Dracon beam. That wasn't to save Bambi, all right?"

"Look, Marco, we are not the only animals around. We, of all people, ought to understand that."

"Cassie, who cares? We're fighting to save the world from the Yeerks. Who cares about some ecology, tree-hugging, recycle-your-cans stuff?"

"I do," I said.

"Well, that's you," Marco said. "Personally, what I care about is the fact that a bunch of

Yeerks have that, that fortress back there, and they're going to use it to tear up these woods looking for us."

I started to say something back, when Jake held up his hand. "It seems to me it doesn't matter whether we have slightly different ideas about *why* we care. I mean, either way, we want to stop this from going on. Right?"

He looked at Marco, then at me. I was annoyed with Jake right then. I mean, I understand that he has to consider everyone's ideas equally. But still, it was like he was agreeing with Marco that it didn't matter if the forest was wiped out, as long as we survived.

I turned to Rachel for support, but she found something to look at down on the ground.

Oh, great, I thought. *Even Rachel thinks I'm wrong.*

<The important thing is we have to stop them,> Tobias said.

"And how exactly do we do that?" Marco asked. "That place is the Fortress of Doom."

"Knock it down? Blow it up?" Rachel mused.

"Grab some of that heavy equipment they have and run it into the place?" Marco suggested. "We don't have the benefit of surprise. They know we're coming. They know sooner or later we're gonna go after them."

<The heavy equipment would be useless,> Ax said. <That building is surrounded by a force field. The equipment would not penetrate it. Neither would we. We would be stopped by the force field and then cut to pieces by the Dracon beams.>

Rachel's lips pressed into a thin line. "So we just give up? That's the plan? We let them go chopping through the woods till they find you, Ax, or Tobias?"

Ax didn't have an answer.

"You know, I wouldn't want to sound like some stupid ecology nut or anything," I said sarcastically. "But the question is: How did the Yeerks ever get permission to start logging in a national forest?"

"Why is that helpful?" Marco asked, even more sarcastically.

"Because sometimes, Marco, there are more subtle ways of doing things. The Yeerks don't control the entire government. Not yet, anyway. So they had to get legal permission. If they didn't have permission they'd have cops and federal agents and TV newspeople all over them. They don't want that."

Marco looked like he had some smart reply to make. Then he said, "Oh."

Jake cocked an eyebrow at his best friend.

"See, Marco, this is why Cassie is a nicer person than you. She could have said, 'They don't want that, *duh*.'"

Marco grinned, despite himself.

Jake winked at me, and I forgave him for acting like Marco was right before. "What do you think we should do?"

I shrugged. I hate having to think of things that might end up getting people hurt or killed. "I guess . . . I mean, okay, um . . . Okay, look, the Yeerks must have gotten to someone. They must have one of their Controllers in some kind of high position. We need to find out who."

<And how do we do that?> Tobias asked.

"I guess . . . " I looked at Jake for help. I knew the answer. I just didn't want to say it. See, when we make plans, we tend to end up in terrible danger later on.

"We have to get inside that building," Jake said for me.

I nodded. The least I could do was agree.

Rachel shook her head. "I don't know any animal big enough to force a way inside that place."

"Not big," I said. "Small. *Very* small."

CHAPTER 7

"Where have you been?" my dad asked me when I finally got back home later that evening. He was in the kitchen, searching the refrigerator.

It kind of took me by surprise. My parents don't usually ask me a lot of questions. Mostly they trust me. And it used to be they *could* trust me. I don't think I'd lied to my parents before becoming an Animorph. Now it's like I'm lying all the time. It's a rotten feeling.

"Oh . . . um, I was just out walking," I said. "Why? Did you need me for something?"

"Oh, yes," my dad said. He was sounding way too solemn, so I knew he wasn't actually serious. That's the way he is. I guess he has a dry sense of

49

humor. That's what Jake says, anyway. He thinks my dad is the funniest man on the planet.

"What is it?"

"Just got a call from the highway patrol. They said this . . . this certain animal . . . is out by the side of the highway, where it cuts through the forest. They say this certain animal seems to have a bad burn."

I didn't like the way he kept saying "certain animal."

"We have to drive out and get it," my dad said. Then he grinned. "Actually, I'll drive. *You* have to get it."

I groaned. There was only one animal in all the world my dad was afraid of. He handled foxes and wolves and even bears. But he would not handle this "certain animal."

"Are you telling me it's a skunk?" I asked.

He nodded. "You have such a way with skunks," he said. "They like you. Besides, I have to go meet with the board of the Dudette Cat Food Corporation tomorrow. I can't show up smelling like skunk."

My mom appeared, climbing up from the basement. She was carrying a six-pack of V-8 juice. "This is all I could find in the pantry," she said.

You see, tomato juice is one of the few things that helps get rid of skunk smell.

"Mom, shouldn't you be the one to help dad with this? I . . . I have very important homework to do."

"Yeah, right," my mom said.

"This is pathetic. You guys are both highly trained veterinarians," I pointed out. "How can you be scared of skunks?"

"I didn't used to be," my father said darkly. "Back before . . . before the *incident*."

"Just because one skunk sprayed you —"

"In the face," he said.

"Just because you had one bad experience —"

"He sprayed me six times in about three seconds," he said. "I smelled for a week. Your mother made me sleep in the barn. Except the other animals there all became agitated, so I had to set up a tent in the yard."

"Then we had to burn the tent," my mother added. She giggled.

"You do have a way with skunks," my father said. "Actually, you have a way with all animals. Come on, you know skunks love you."

"A burned skunk by the side of a highway loves no one," I said.

Ten minutes later, we were on the highway. We were driving in our new pickup truck. My father's old, beloved pickup truck had been stolen and totally destroyed.

At least that's what my dad believed. Actually, we'd sort of had to borrow it in this terrible battle. Marco had been driving, and Marco cannot drive. The truck had ended up a total wreck in a ditch.

On the way, we listened to the CD player. That was the only thing my dad liked about the new truck. He was playing some old jazz or something.

We reached the spot the highway patrol had told my dad about. We pulled over and put on the hazard lights.

"Careful. People drive like maniacs through here," he warned me as we climbed out.

Cars were blowing past at seventy miles an hour with their high beams on. The black forest pressed in around the road on both sides. I shone a flashlight around the edge of the trees.

Normally, the forest doesn't bother me. But I knew that we were actually within a quarter mile of the Yeerk logging camp. It was beyond strange to be practically going back to the place where, just an hour before, I'd nearly been killed.

It took us at least twenty minutes, walking up and down the grassy shoulder of the road, before my flashlight beam landed on a shock of black and white.

"Dad! Here!"

He came trotting over and added his light to mine. "Yep," he commented. "I'll get the cage.

Don't forget your gloves. You know skunks are a major vector for rabies."

"Dad, I have had the shot."

"No vaccine is a hundred percent," he said.

I walked toward the skunk. It saw me and turned tiny, glittering black eyes on me.

"Don't be afraid," I said, pitching my voice high. "It's okay. We're here to help you. It's going to be just fine."

Here's the thing about skunks: They are the sweetest animals alive. They don't have a mean bone in their bodies. But that's because they don't have to be mean. They possess the ultimate weapon.

Even so, they will always warn you. If they turn their backs on you, that's a warning. If they raise their tails with the tips down, that's a very *serious* warning. If they raise the tips of their tails . . . you are in a very bad situation.

If you're dealing with a skunk who has turned buttward and raised its tail all the way, you would want to freeze. Trust me. Every wild animal knows this. Dogs, unfortunately, don't understand about skunks, but bears, raccoons, wolves, and most birds of prey know that you just don't mess with that skunk tail.

Maybe you think you know how bad skunk musk is because you've driven by skunk roadkill. That's nothing. Up close and personal, it's a whole different level of stench. If you imagine the most horrible smell possible, then multiply it by a thousand, you still won't be close.

"It's okay, sweetie," I cooed. "Don't spray me. I'm your friend, so please don't spray me."

I moved closer and crouched lower, making myself small. I wanted to look nonthreatening. I moved very slowly, a step at a time, always cooing and baby-talking like I was going to grab a little kid armed with a shotgun.

The skunk moved! I froze.

The skunk settled back down. I breathed again.

"Please don't spray me," I said. I reached into my pocket and took out a bit of mouse meat. We keep frozen mice for the raptors we handle. Skunks also enjoy a nice mouse or grasshopper as part of their diets.

"Here you go. Dinner."

I held the meat out for the skunk. The skunk didn't seem to be hungry, but it did accept the fact that I must be okay if I was offering dinner.

I crouched beside the skunk and set my flashlight on the ground. Carefully, with my gloved hand, I reached out to touch the animal.

It was shaking. Shivering. And, at that very moment, I could see why.

There was a burn right across the skunk's

back. A perfectly semicircular burn, as if someone had simply sliced a scoop out of it.

"Dracon beam," I whispered. "You were there, weren't you? Poor baby."

Aiming at me and Marco, the Yeerks had hit this skunk instead. A completely innocent animal caught in the cross fire of the war between Yeerks and humans.

The Yeerks would destroy all the forest and all its animals to get at us.

"Sorry," I whispered to the skunk.

I lifted it slowly, carefully, up into my arms.

CHAPTER 8

We met at the mall. It was a Saturday, so it was a normal place we might be.

When you live in a world where you're surrounded by possible enemies, it's important not to do anything too unusual. You don't want to draw attention.

Not even from your own family and school friends. You just never know who can be trusted and who can't.

The Yeerks believed we were Andalites. We wanted them to go on believing that. If they ever figured out we were humans, let alone kids, we were toast.

So we left no clues. We tried not to act like we were a group. We didn't want some Controller teacher or whatever thinking, "Hey, you know what? Those same kids are always hanging out together, acting like they're planning something."

We had to look and act and seem normal. Rachel still went to gymnastics classes and shopped. Jake and Marco still shot hoops in Jake's driveway or played video games. I took care of animals at the Wildlife Rehabilitation Clinic.

There was nothing we could do to make Tobias seem normal. He was way past being normal. But Tobias came from a terrible, messed-up background, shuttling from one indifferent aunt or uncle to another. He'd never really been part of a family or a structure, and sadly, no one seemed to notice when he simply disappeared.

I spent an hour wandering along behind Rachel as she moved like a professional through the racks at The Limited and Banana Republic and The Gap *and* the various department stores.

Rachel has some bizarre, supernatural instinct for when and where sales will happen. She doesn't need the advertising. She just "knows."

We were cruising through a series of tables piled with sweaters at Express. Rachel was looking for a particular shade of green that probably didn't exist.

"What do you think we're going to do?" I asked her.

She looked up from fondling a sweater. "What? Oh. I guess we'll probably go in. If we can find a way."

"That's what I was wondering. What way? How do we get inside that place? I mean, I know we're thinking insect morph. But if anyone is planning on doing ants again, I'll tell you right now, I'm not doing it."

Rachel gave a little shudder. "I'm sure no one wants to do ants again."

We'd had some really bad experiences morphing. But morphing ants was the worst. We ended up being the wrong species and tribe of ants in the middle of enemy ant territory.

You would not believe the nightmares that came out of that one. The tunnels pressing in all around, and then hundreds of vicious ant soldiers exploded all around us, attacking, attacking . . .

"No ants," I said. I looked at Rachel, trying to catch her eye. "Right?"

Rachel shrugged. Then she glanced at her watch. "It's time. Ax is coming with them, so let's not keep them waiting."

"Ax? Uh-oh."

Jake, Marco, and a strikingly handsome boy were all sitting in the food court. They seemed to be arguing loudly about who had won some video game in the arcade.

"Hey! Rachel!" Marco called out as we passed by. "What are you guys doing here?"

I really didn't like this kind of acting. It seemed silly to me. But it had to look like an accident that we all ended up together in the same place at the same time.

"We're shopping," I muttered. "You know how I love shopping."

"Why don't you guys hang out with us. Have some of our nachos," Jake said, smiling brightly.

I looked at the paper plate of nachos. They were completely gone. There was nothing left but a paper plate with a slight orange stain from the cheese. There was a matching orange stain on the chin of the very handsome boy between Marco and Jake.

Jake saw what I was looking at and rolled his eyes. "At least he didn't eat the plate this time."

"Hello," Ax said to me. "I am Jake's cousin, Phillip. Jake's cousin. Scousin. Scuzzin. I am from out of town."

I couldn't help but laugh. Ax had long ago created a human morph out of DNA he'd acquired from the four of us. He was a weird blending of each of us. He was male, but sort of pretty in a weird way.

He looked like a human. He basically *was* a human. But he still had a lot of problems adjusting to the human morph. For one thing, since Andalites have no mouth, he found his human mouth utterly fascinating. He couldn't help but play with the sounds of words.

And the boy was dangerous around food.

"Were the nachos good?" I asked him.

"They tasted of grease and salt. Plus, there was another flavor that reminds me of some delicious engine oil I tried once. Oil. Oil-luh."

"Engine oil?" Jake asked. "Ax . . . I mean, Phillip . . . You know how I mentioned you can't eat cigarette butts or dryer lint? Add engine oil to the list."

Ax nodded. "Yes. There are many rules for eating."

Marco pushed out a chair for me to sit in. "Okay, if we're done with the little side trip into the bizarre-o zone, let's deal with business."

"Tobias came by this morning," Jake said, keeping his voice low. "He watched the place from high up. He thinks the Controllers at the site have little transponders on their belts that let them pass through the force field."

"So we just have to grab a transponder," Rachel said.

"No," Ax said. "The transponder would be keyed to the biochemical signature of the wearer. The Yeerks are not as —"

"Don't say that word," Jake hissed.

I saw Marco's eyes dart quickly, looking to see if anyone was close enough to have overheard.

"Sorry. Ree. Saw-ree," Ax said. "Rachel's plan would not work."

Jake sighed. "Tobias also saw something else. Inside the force field. There are tiny holes in the wood foundation of the building. He thinks it's termites at work."

"Termites?" I asked.

Jake nodded. "Yep."

I swallowed. "Jake, termites are awfully close to being ants."

"They aren't as vicious," Jake said. "I looked up some information on the Internet. Besides, if we make sure we morph a termite from that very colony, we'd fit right in."

I was having trouble breathing. I noticed Marco's face turning gray. Even Ax looked grim.

"You're not serious, right?" I asked Jake. "I mean, termites? Termites?"

I probably sounded slightly hysterical. I know I *felt* slightly hysterical.

"I don't know how else to do it," Jake said. He was looking down at the table and biting his lip. "Cassie, you were right when you said the real question is how these guys got permission to start logging. That's their weakness. We *have* to know how they pulled this off. To know that we *have* to get inside that building."

61

"Through termite tunnels?" Marco asked. "Look, how do we even get a termite to acquire? They're all inside that force field, right?"

I wanted that to be the truth. But when I looked at Jake, he just shook his head a little. "Tobias says they were working on the building a little today. Putting in extra Dracon beams. They had to cut away some of the logs."

Jake reached into the pocket of his jacket. He pulled out a small, glass vial. The top had tiny holes in it to let air through.

Inside the vial was a tiny, tan-and-white bug. It was about the size of an ant. It had an enlarged brown head.

"Same colony," Jake said. "From the same building."

I stared at the termite. It tried to climb up the side of the glass, but it slipped back down.

It was helpless. It was trapped in what must have seemed like a huge glass cell held by a creature so gigantic that the termite could never even begin to imagine it.

Jake took the top off the vial.

"We don't do this unless everyone agrees," he said. "But we can't let the . . . *them* . . . start tearing through the forest."

Rachel held out her hand. Jake tapped the vial till the insect landed in her palm.

I saw it crawl across Rachel's lifeline. And I

saw it become still, as Rachel acquired the termite DNA.

I imagined being that termite. Crawling across the gigantic hand. Thinking every crease in Rachel's palm was as deep as a ditch.

When Rachel was done, I held out my own hand. It was shaking. It was shaking and I couldn't stop it from shaking.

The brightly lit mall food court suddenly seemed dark.

Lord, that tiny insect scared me.

Deep down inside, it truly scared me.

CHAPTER 9

We would go that night. That very night.

We were supposed to use the afternoon to deal with chores and family stuff and homework.

Try it sometime. Try doing homework when you think you may be going to your doom in a few hours. Try concentrating on math when you're thinking you have to turn into a termite and sneak into a heavily defended building.

Good luck.

I went out to the barn. My dad was out there, making his rounds. He didn't need my help, but he didn't say no, either.

"Did you finish your homework?"

"Mostly." I added another lie to the pile I'd already had to tell.

"I was going to take a closer look at your skunk from last night. She was very agitated so I had to give her a mild sedative."

"It's a female?"

"Yep."

My father carried the cage into the little side room he uses to examine the patients. I eased the skunk from her cage and cradled her out to the examination table. She seemed very calm now, but it was an unnatural, drugged calm.

The night before, my dad had bandaged the wound and now he carefully removed the gauze. The sight of the burn made me wince, even though I've seen hundreds of injured animals.

"Hmm. Hmm. Pah. Pah. Pah. Hmmm."

That's the sound my dad makes when he's examining something interesting. "Pah." I don't know why, he just does.

"Weird. Very unusual. I cannot for the life of me guess what caused this burn. It's too neat. Too clean. The only good thing is, whatever caused it was so hot it partially cauterized the tissue."

"Muscle damage, or is it just superficial?" I asked.

My dad glanced at me and smiled. "It's mostly fur and skin that were burned. But I see some moderately severe damage in the shoulder here. Much deeper and the spine would have

65

been burned. But she'll live. I wish I could say as much for her kits."

"Her what? She has babies?"

"Yeah. I'd say probably about six, seven weeks old."

"She has babies? Out there somewhere in the woods?"

My dad started applying a new bandage. "Cassie, you know nature plays rough."

"But they're too young to survive on their own, aren't they?"

"I can't be sure," he said, not looking at me.

It occurred to me then that sometimes maybe he lied to me, too. For my own good. Or because of what he thought was my own good.

"They're sitting in some den wondering where their mother is," I said. "They'll starve to death. Or be eaten by predators."

"Hand me the scissors," my father said.

"Yeah. Okay. Um, look. I meant to ask you, is it okay if I spend the night at Rachel's tonight?"

"Sure, honey. You know, if your mom says it's okay. Hey. You never asked how my meeting went with the cat food people this morning. We got some additional funding!"

We talked for a while as we made rounds together. But my heart wasn't in it. I was thinking about some baby skunks somewhere, mewing and crying for their mother.

And I was thinking I wished my dad wasn't so quick to let me go to Rachel's. Because, of course, we weren't really having a sleepover. Rachel was going to tell her mom she was spending the night at my house. And Jake would tell his parents a lie, and Marco would tell his father a lie, and we'd all be going into a situation that none of us wanted to be in.

I was going to face death, that very night. And the last thing I would have said to my father was a lie.

I remembered the tunnels of the ants. I remembered them the way I saw them in my nightmares. I never had *seen* them in reality. Ants don't see very well, and there's no light underground.

But in my dreams I saw everything. I saw the huge, metallic-looking heads of the enemy ants as they crashed through sand walls and locked their massive pincers on me and tried to slice me into pieces.

Do you know what it's like to think that you're going to die, and never even get back to human form? To believe that you're going to die as an *ant*, trapped in a hell that no human had ever been to?

And now I also saw those little skunk kits. Starving. Crying out, and with each cry, signaling to some predator.

"Sweetheart, are you okay?"

I realized my dad was staring at me. I had been breathing hard, almost crying. There were beads of sweat on my forehead.

"Yeah. Fine. Fine," I said quietly.

He finished his rounds and left.

I stayed behind. I went back to the skunk in her cage.

I opened the cage door and put my hand in. I was not wearing a glove.

See, you can't acquire DNA if you're wearing gloves.

CHAPTER 10

"Well, what a surprise seeing you all here," Marco said in a low whisper.

"Everyone still up for this?" Jake asked.

"Sure," Marco answered. "We're looking forward to it. Who needs sleep when you can run off on a suicide mission instead?"

It was pitch-black. It was three in the morning. We were at the edge of the forest. Jake, Rachel, Marco, and me. Tobias was in the tree above us.

The same five kids who had wandered stupidly through a construction site at night on our way home from the mall. The same kids who had seen the Andalite fighter land. The same five kids whose lives had been changed forever.

We had been made into soldiers that night. Soldiers in a terrible war we could not really hope to win.

Tobias had paid a terrible price. But so had the rest of us. There we were, in the dark, ready to do things that would make us scream if we ever stopped to think about them for too long.

Ax was there, too. Poor Ax, who was even more alone than the rest of us. He was in his own body, his stalk eyes restlessly peering in every direction.

"I thought we'd morph owls," Jake suggested. "They're fast, and they fly well at night. Till we get close."

I was relieved. Owl was a good choice for what I had in mind. Owls are the only natural predators of adult skunks. See, some species of owls don't have a sense of smell. If you're going to eat skunks, that's a good thing.

I wasn't going to eat adult skunks, of course. I was going to try to find some skunk babies.

<Wish I could go with you guys,> Tobias said. <But I'm not much use at night.>

"You found us the way to get into this place," Jake said. "And you got us the termite to morph."

"And we're just so amazingly grateful," Marco said sarcastically.

We all laughed nervously. It was good to know that the others were all as scared as I was.

We all started to remove our outer clothing. We wore our morphing suits underneath — a collection of bike shorts, leotards, and T-shirts. We can morph skintight clothing, but not things like sweaters or shoes or watches.

Jake wore a pair of bike shorts and a sort of spandex top. Marco snickered.

"What?" Jake demanded.

Marco put on an innocent face. "Nothing. Nothing. I'm just saying if we're going to be superheroes we need to do something about these stupid outfits. We look like refugees from a Bulgarian gymnastics competition. That's all I'm saying."

"Except for Rachel, of course," I pointed out. Naturally, Rachel had found a way to coordinate her outfit. She looked great.

"Here's the plan," Jake said. "We morph owls to get close. We demorph at least two hundred yards away from the compound. Then we crawl close, morph termites, dig under the force field, and enter the termite holes in the outside of the building."

"As long as it's nice and simple," Rachel said darkly. She looked at me, and I realized that even fearless Rachel was afraid.

That scared me.

I tried to focus entirely on assuming the owl morph. But my brain was buzzing away. You know how sometimes you can't stop your brain from just racing around? It's like a computer that's playing a dozen programs at once.

I was worrying about too many things — about my science project, lying to my parents, whether Ax really tried drinking engine oil, whether the baby skunks had already been killed. . . .

Maybe it was self-defense. I didn't want to start worrying about the thing that *really* worried me.

Somehow my life had turned very, very weird.

I saw Ax was morphing quickly. His tail went limp, like an empty sock. Feathers were growing to replace his fur.

I looked down at my own arm and saw the feather patterns being drawn on my skin. They were beautiful, really, if you didn't stop to think about them being on you. You could see the quill, a gently curved shaft. From it the thousands of individual vanes spread.

Then, quite suddenly, the feather-drawing became three-dimensional. They seemed to simply pop out of my skin. It itched a little as the feathers grew out, all across my body.

I was shrinking all the while. Getting smaller

and smaller. The dirt and pine needles and leaves and twigs all came rushing up at me.

My bare feet grew rough, as if they were one big callous. Toes melted together, then formed into talons. Long, curved, sharp, tearing claws grew.

The talons were the main killing weapon of the great horned owl. An owl would fly along, silent in the night. Then it would strike, grabbing the prey — a rabbit, a squirrel, a rat, a skunk — by the head. . . .

The bones all through my body were rearranging themselves. Many disappeared altogether. Others became twisted and misshapen. My breast bone grew deeper. My various finger bones grew longer first, then shorter. All of this made a grinding noise that resonated up through my body.

My internal organs were radically redesigned. And my eyes seemed to swell and swell till they filled my entire head. My eyes were so huge compared to my body that they practically rubbed together inside my skull.

Suddenly, it was no longer night. It was as bright as day.

The amount of light that was a dim, flickering candle to my human eyes was a spotlight to my owl's eyes.

<Whoa!> I heard Rachel cry.

<I enjoy these eyes very much,> Ax commented. <They are wonderful.>

I spread my arms wide and opened my wings. The change was complete. I felt the cold edge of the owl's instincts. The instincts of a predator.

I had morphed the owl before, so I knew what to expect. I had used the eyes and the wings and felt the brain. It wasn't exactly second nature, but at least it wasn't a surprise.

<Ready?> Jake asked.

I flapped my wings and drew up my feet and rose easily into the tree branches that, in the darkness, were invisible to humans, but clear as blazing neon to me.

I saw Tobias sitting perched on his branch. I felt his instinctive hawk's caution as a flight of five horned owls flew past.

The day belonged to the hawks. But night was ours.

<Good luck,> Tobias said. <Don't eat anything I wouldn't eat.>

<Hah-hah,> Marco laughed. He was high on the thrill of a good morph. So was I, I guess. There is a rush of power that comes from being an animal in its natural element. Particularly a predator.

In the air at night, nothing could touch us. We reigned supreme in the forest.

We flew in a loose formation, not soaring

above the trees, but flitting through them. Our wings didn't make a sound. An owl's wings are as carefully designed as the wings of the most advanced stealth fighter. More, really. The feathers are designed not to flutter or ruffle as the owl glides through the still night air.

Frightened mice, listening for any possible danger, hear nothing at all as the owl swoops down for the kill.

As well as I could see, I could also hear everything. I could hear as well as the wolves.

As we flew to what might be our destruction, I tried to focus on my other goal — listening for the cries of skunk kits. Watching the ground below for the waddling, shuffling walk of a lost baby skunk.

<This is so weird,> Marco said. <I love this part. It's the next part I'm not looking forward to at all.>

<It'll be okay,> Jake said.

<Yeah, I mean, what could possibly go wrong?> Rachel asked dryly.

I swooped and zoomed through the trees. All the while I watched the ground below me and focused my hearing, and in that way I reached the Yeerk compound without having to think too much about what was coming next.

CHAPTER 11

lmost there,> Jake said. <Another couple of minutes.>

Even in thought-speak I could hear the tension in his voice. I felt something like a cold hand squeezing my heart.

Then . . .

A noise. A noise against a background of noises. But this noise was one that the owl's brain *wanted* to hear. A noise the owl's brain had evolved to notice. The sound of helplessness. The sound of a weak creature. Weak, tiny, helpless babies.

There! It was coming from a hole that no other animal would have seen in the pitch-black of night. A hole dug beneath the roots of a thorn-bush.

Four . . . no, five separate voices. Were they the skunk kits? Maybe. I couldn't be sure. But it was night, and they sounded like they were alone. It could be.

I looked around, swiveling my owl's neck. I tried to form a picture of the place. The trees. The outcropping of rocks just twenty feet away. I wanted to be able to find the place again.

If I was still around to find anything.

The mewling sound of the babies reached something inside me. Inside the human Cassie. But to the owl it was the sound of a meal.

It's strange to have those two feelings in your head at the same time — human compassion and the cold ruthlessness of the predator. Strange.

<Okay,> Jake said, a few seconds later. <Here.>

We swooped low and landed. I started to de-morph quickly. I didn't want to feel that predator in my mind anymore. Not right then.

The world went dark as my human eyes reemerged. The forest was a darker, quieter place to Homo sapiens.

I looked around and couldn't see any of the landmarks I'd tried to spot. I would never find those skunk kits in the dark. Not with human eyes, anyway. Maybe by the light of day. I could come back in the morning.

If . . .

"Okay, we have to get as close to the edge of that compound as we can," Jake whispered. "We can't be spotted as humans. But we can't morph termites too far from the building. Termites don't exactly move fast."

<I have a suggestion, Prince Jake,> Ax said.

Ax is under the impression that Jake is the equivalent of an Andalite prince.

<A distraction,> he continued. <We could give the Yeerks something to chase.>

I knew instantly what he had in mind. "An Andalite?" I asked him.

<The Yeerks would not be able to resist,> he said.

"You could end up very dead that way," Marco said.

"No, Ax," Jake said. "We need you inside. There may be Yeerk computers in there. We need you. But a distraction isn't a bad idea." Jake looked at me. "Anyone want to volunteer? It would probably be safer than going inside."

He was offering me a way out. A way to avoid having to become a termite. I should have said yes. I wanted to say yes.

But I couldn't do it. I couldn't take the easier way out.

"Okay, we draw straws. All except Ax. He goes in, regardless."

Jake pulled up four strands of tall grass. He shortened them all to about six inches. Then, he took one and shortened it further. "Short straw plays tag with the Yeerks."

He concealed the bottoms of the straws in his fist.

"Next time let's play some other game," Marco said as he drew a straw. "Yahtzee, maybe. I don't like games that involve life and death."

One after the other, we each drew a straw. A long straw. I looked carefully at the straw in my hand. Yes, it was a long one.

Jake looked shocked. He held the short straw.

We were all shocked. Somehow it just seemed automatic that Jake would be there with us.

Marco grinned. "Sooner or later we had to try a mission without you, oh great and fearless leader."

Marco could joke about it. But none of us felt right going in without Jake. Now it was too late to change that.

"Okay," Jake said briskly. "You guys know what to do. I'll use the wolf morph. The Yeerks will be on the lookout for wolves."

79

He started to walk away. Then he stopped and looked back. "Be careful, all right?"

"Go ahead, *Mom*," Rachel said. "We can handle this."

"At least we *hope* we can," I muttered.

Jake walked away and was quickly out of sight.

"Okay, we have to be ready as soon as Jake starts making trouble," Rachel said. "We hear something go down, we run toward the perimeter of the compound, staying just back in the trees, morph, and hope we can find the way to the building."

<What do you know about these termites we are morphing?> Ax wondered.

"They're like ants," Marco said.

"Actually, they're related to cockroaches," I said. "I looked them up in one of my mom's books. They have a society like ants, but roaches are closer relatives. They eat cellulose — the stuff in wood. Bacteria in their guts digest the wood. The worker termites . . . they, um, they eliminate their waste. And the soldier termites kind of eat it. I think, judging from the termite Tobias brought us, that we are going to be morphing soldier termites."

The three of them were staring at me, looking a little sick.

"Well, Ax wanted to know," I said.

A light!

"Look!" I hissed. "Way off through the woods. That must be on the far side of the compound. The spotlights just went on."

We could hear the sounds of human voices yelling. And then, the wild, defiant howl of a wolf.

"That's it. Let's rock," Rachel said.

We ran toward the compound. We ran, hunched low, scurrying from tree to bush. Then, as we got still closer, we dropped down and crawled on all fours.

I heard shouting and the eerie zap of Dracon beams being fired.

"I hope he's okay," I whispered. I didn't think anyone could hear me.

But Ax said, <Prince Jake is very smart. He will be fine.>

"Do you guys think we're close enough now?" Marco wondered.

We were closer than we had been the day before. Just a few feet from the edge of the clearing. All of us hunched down behind one large tree trunk. Even Ax, which, in his normal state, is awkward for him.

We huddled close, like some big group hug. When we morphed we would become tiny. And even a few feet between us would seem like a mile.

"Time to go termite," Rachel said. She had her arm around my back.

I was already sick with fear. Afraid for Jake. Afraid for my friends. Afraid of the very thing I was about to become.

"Can I just say that this sucks?" I muttered.

"Amen," Marco agreed. We were shoulder to shoulder. My head touched his.

And then, as my very bones rattled and my teeth chattered from fear, I began the process that would dissolve my bones, and melt away my teeth.

Down, down, down.

Falling . . . falling forever. It was like I had jumped off the Empire State Building and was falling. Yet even though I fell, I never quite hit the ground.

I was going from a girl of less than five feet to an insect less than a quarter of an inch long. I was becoming something that could have crawled inside my own ear.

Already the others who had been so close seemed to be a long way off. With my eyes still mostly human, I could see Rachel's face lose its features, and bulge out. I saw the monstrously big mandibles spring like black, sideways tusks from her mouth.

And then, my eyes went dark.

I was blind.

And I was glad.

CHAPTER 12

I couldn't see, but I could *feel* the antennae as they extruded from my forehead.

I couldn't see, but I could *feel* the extra set of legs growing from my sides.

I could sense, rather than see, that my head was huge compared to the rest of my body.

I could sense that I had a swollen abdomen.

I could feel the massive pincers where my mouth had been.

I wanted to scream. I wanted to scream so badly, but I no longer had a voice. I no longer had a tongue.

I was less than a quarter of an inch long. I was as long as any two or three letters on this page. Grains of sand were the size of bowling balls to me. With my wildly waving feelers I could sense a huge, long shaft, like a fallen log. It was over my head. I slowly realized that it was a single pine needle.

I waited for the termite's instincts and mind to suddenly surge within my own. But the termite brain — such as it was — wasn't saying anything. It was totally silent.

My senses brought me almost nothing. I was blind. I could feel vibrations from sound, but they were vague. The termite's sense of "hearing" was not as good as its relative, the cockroach. I knew. I had been a cockroach.

All I had was a sense of smell. Or something like smell that came from my antennae waving in the air.

<Everyone okay?> I asked shakily. I desperately wanted to talk to someone. Anyone. I needed to know the others were alive.

<Yeah,> Rachel answered. <I guess I am okay. It's just that I can't see anything.>

<Termites are blind, except for the queens and kings,> I said. I must have sounded much calmer than I felt.

<These are very strange creatures,> Ax commented. <I feel no instincts. It's as if they are just a body. A machine.>

<Well, let's get these bodies outta here,>

Marco said. <Sooner or later the Yeerks are going to get tired of chasing Jake around the woods.>

<Which way?> Rachel asked. <Slight problem — we're totally blind.>

<I . . . maybe I'm crazy, but I get this sense . . . this feeling . . . like something is calling to me,> I explained.

<Okay, maybe,> Marco said. <I have the same feeling. Like someone yelling from a long way off.>

<Let's follow that. Whatever it is,> Rachel said. <It's as good a direction as any.>

I set out toward the vague, distant voice. I had no idea if the others were going in the same direction. I guess they were all within a few inches of me, but I couldn't tell.

The termite legs were not very strong or very fast. Not as fast as an ant's. I could feel the rocks I was climbing over. Or the grains of dirt, I guess they were. They felt like rocks, anyway. Jagged, sharp-edged crystals, seemingly as big as a human head.

I motored on all six legs, trying hard not to think about anything but moving forward. *Just keep moving,* I told myself. *Don't think about how small and defenseless you are.*

<Hey. I feel something,> Rachel said. <It's . . . I guess it must be the edge of the force field.>

At the same time I reached the force field myself. I felt it as a tingling hum that vibrated my tiny body. I could feel the rocks around me vibrating. I could feel the very air around me dancing.

<At least we're going in the right direction,> Marco pointed out.

I moved closer to the invisible wall of snapping, humming power. Suddenly I realized my legs were just motoring away but I wasn't going anywhere.

<We will have to dig under it,> Ax said. <It will stop at the top layer of dirt.>

<Does someone know how to make these pathetic bodies dig?> Rachel asked snappishly.

I flattened myself down and tried wiggling between two big grains of dirt. It didn't work. Then I sensed one of those hugely long logs suspended in the air not far away. A pine needle.

I shuffled over toward it. The pine needle was close to the ground, but there was still plenty of room for me beneath it.

<Hey!> I yelled, genuinely excited. <Find a pine needle or something that crosses the line. I think maybe there's no force field directly beneath them.>

<Yes,> Ax agreed. <The pine needle may cast a shadow in the force field.>

I reached up for the pine needle with my antennae and felt my way along beneath it. I could feel the tingly edges of the force field on either side of me. But the pine needle did cast a sort of shadow. And within that shadow, I could squeeze through.

<I'm through!> I said. At the same time, I became aware that the vague, far-off "voice" I'd heard calling to me was much stronger.

For a weird moment I actually thought it was my mother's voice. And I wanted to go toward it.

I moved my six legs and headed across the landscape of dirt boulders. I was sure where I was going now. I could hear the voice in my head. I could hear the call.

My termite body seemed to be moving on its own now. It was like I was a passenger in a car that someone else was driving.

<Is everyone through?> I asked.

<Yes,> Rachel said.

She sounded distracted to me. Like she was listening to someone else and didn't want me interrupting. But that was okay, because I didn't really want to talk to her, either.

I quickly covered the ground to the building. I didn't *see* that it was the building, you understand. I just knew. And the terrible thing is, I never even paused to wonder *how* I knew.

<What are we . . . > Marco's voice. He didn't finish his thought. I didn't care.

<Guys?> Rachel asked. <Um . . . >

The opening was just ahead. I knew it was there. I knew that other soldier termites would be guarding the entrance.

I felt no fear.

I clambered up from the dirt into the tunnel opening. Familiar smells. Smells I knew. Home. Home. My place. Where I was from, and where I belonged.

I smelled the other soldiers with my antennae. They touched me with their antennae, as I did to them. We were of the colony.

The colony.

I raced swiftly down the tunnel. It headed upward at a sharp angle, but the angle meant little to me. I weighed practically nothing. A worker was ahead of me. It extruded a pellet of digested cellulose. Wood pulp. I quickly gobbled it up.

Within the wood pulp food there were messages. Hormones passing through the colony, containing information. Vague orders. Indistinct yet powerful instructions.

I was now caught up in a rush of workers off to obey the voiceless voice in their heads. Some were off to chew a new tunnel. Others were off to the egg chamber to rotate the eggs.

And I had my orders, too.

I raced along tunnels lined with chewed and

digested wood pulp. Tunnels cut through the dried wood that supported the building.

I felt side tunnels open on one side, then the next. A tunnel above. Air flowed faint — but fresh — actually creating a tiny breeze.

There was no light. None. But it didn't matter because I was blind. I was blind, but I was not lost.

What am I doing? an alien voice asked.

I ignored it.

NO! the voice cried.

I had heard the voice before. But it came from far away and it spoke a language I didn't understand.

NO! NO! NO! Let me go!

I felt a queasy, sickening feeling inside me.

But still I powered down the tunnel, turning here, turning there. Always moving toward a goal. There was a powerful smell. It was growing stronger and stronger.

I went to it. I *had* to go to it.

NO! Let me go! Let me go!

Down the black tunnels. Over and through the packed rush-hour streams of workers. To the center. To the core. To the heart.

Help me! Help me! the voice screamed.

The voice . . . my voice.

The faint, failing voice of the human named Cassie.

Me.

Me!

Ahhhhhhhhh!

Suddenly, I was Cassie again. I knew my name. I knew who I was.

But it no longer mattered. The termite body was out of my control. A stronger will than mine was guiding it.

The termite suddenly emerged into a vast, open space. A space that in reality was no more than two or three inches across. And yet it felt like an auditorium to me.

Suddenly I knew who had seized control of the termite brain.

I knew who had brushed my human mind aside.

She was vast. Huge beyond belief. At one end I sensed the termite head and useless, waving termite arms. From that small head and body there extended a monstrous, pulsating sack. As big as a blimp.

At the far end was a double row of sticky, slimy eggs, to be picked up and carried away by worker termites.

The queen.

I was in the chamber of the termite queen.

CHAPTER 13

The queen!

I could feel her power. This was *her* world. These were all *her* slaves. More than slaves — they had no will of their own.

I knew who I was again. But I felt weak and pathetic. I was unable to control the termite body I was in. That body belonged to *her*.

She had orders for me — protect the egg-carrying worker termites. The orders came in smells and vague feelings, but they were impossible to refuse.

<Rachel,> I called. <Marco. Ax.>

<I . . . > It was Rachel's thought-speak voice. <I . . . I . . . Oh, no. No! No!>

<Rachel! It's the queen. She's controlling us,> I said.

<I can't . . . my body . . . it just . . . >

<Marco! Marco can you hear me? Marco!>

<She's got me. I can't say no. I can't stop!> he cried in anguished response.

My own body motored away on its six legs. I fell in step behind two workers. Each was carrying one of the gooey, precious eggs. I had to protect them. There might be enemies. We walked along the grotesque length of the queen. Toward her head.

Ants. They were the enemy. Sometimes they came. Sometimes they poured down the tunnels, looking for the eggs, to carry them off for food.

Sometimes they attacked the queen herself. The soldiers fought them. The soldiers sometimes died fighting them.

<The queen!> Rachel's voice said. <The only way . . . destroy the queen.>

It was like an electric jolt in my mind! Get rid of the queen! Yes. The only way. They wouldn't be expecting that. There would be no one to stop me!

But my body was not my own. I could not make it . . .

The two workers plodded along before me. I could feel their hind ends with my feelers. And I knew the queen's head was just to my right. Just a half inch. Less.

The queen's head . . . feelers . . . eyes . . . like an ant!

One chance . . . focus . . . focus . . . I had to trick the termite mind. I had to draw on every ounce of my strength.

If I failed, I would live out the rest of my life as a mindless slave of the termite queen.

Now! Do it now!

I swerved right. It was like moving through molasses. The queen had ordered me to go after the workers, and I was disobeying.

Ant! Ant! I screamed the word in my own head. *Ant! Destroy! Destroy! Destroy the ant!*

I clambered over a half dozen termites who were tending the queen.

I could feel my will weakening. I couldn't get rid of the queen. I had to kill an *ant*. That was my purpose — to keep ants away from the queen.

I scampered toward the queen's head. I felt my antennae touch her. I opened my massive pincer jaws. . . .

Termites ran around insanely. They were racing, out of control, lost, confused. For a moment I did the same. The queen was gone.

I think in some way I wanted to forget who I was. What I had done. I wanted to become one of the lost, panicked termites.

<We're free! We're out! Cassie, where are

93

you? Get out of there!> I heard a far-off voice cry. Was it Ax? Marco? Rachel?

<Demorph!> I cried with my last shred of control.

<No! Cassie, no!> a voice screamed in my head. <You're inside a piece of wood!>

<Demorph!> I screamed again. Human. I wanted to be human again. Let me be human! Let me out of this place. Out of this body.

I grew. Walls pressed in around me. I filled the tunnel. I couldn't grow anymore!

Trapped! Pain. Nothing but pain! I was a swollen, vast termite. Larger than any queen. Huge.

I couldn't grow anymore. And I couldn't stop. I was trying to become human again, to fit a human body into a space no bigger than the inside of a walnut.

Then . . . explosion!

The walls opened up. Splinters! Fresh air rushed across my hard termite skin. My head was free of the wood and growing. But my body was still trapped. Squeezing with terrible pain.

I had eyes now. They could see, but only dimly. I was still tiny, and in the air above me a huge blade as long as a passenger jet slashed downward. The wood splintered again and my body was free.

I grew and grew. Arms . . . legs . . . my own head.

I was on my knees on a wooden floor. Marco and Rachel stood over me. Ax had used his tail to slice open the wood. They had all escaped the colony. They had demorphed.

It was dark in the room, but there were glowing red-and-green indicator lights. And there was a computer monitor showing neat screen-saver triangles floating and reforming.

"Are you okay?" Rachel asked. She bent down and put her hand on my shoulder.

I gave her a hug. Then, just as suddenly, I pushed her away. "Let me go! Don't touch me! Don't touch me! DON'T TOUCH ME!"

Rachel was on me in a flash. She clamped her hand over my mouth. Marco grabbed my ankles and held them still.

"Cassie!" Rachel hissed. "Shut up. We're inside the Yeerk building. We're in a side room, but we can hear people in the next room!"

I was beyond caring. I struggled and fought and tried to scream.

"Ax, whatever you can do with that computer, do it!" Marco whispered urgently.

Rachel and Marco held me pinned against the floor. And slowly . . . very slowly . . . my bunched muscles relaxed. I stopped fighting.

"Are you okay now?" Rachel asked.

Okay? I would never be okay again. But I nodded my head anyway. Rachel took her hand away from my mouth.

"It's over, Cassie," Marco said. "You saved us. It's over. And we have other problems now."

"I'm good," I said. "I'm fine." But my skin was crawling. Evil, terrible memories were crowding in on me.

<I have access,> Ax said. <Accessing. Um . . . Marco or Rachel, I need a human to help me understand the meaning of what I am seeing here.>

Marco climbed up off the floor. Rachel stayed with me. She was stroking my hair, like my mom would have done if I'd had a nightmare.

It was hard to think of Rachel as being nurturing. But she did the right thing.

I heard sounds in the next room. Human voices. And Hork-Bajir, speaking their weird mix of their own native tongue and human speech they'd learned for duty on Earth.

"Some kind of commission," Marco mused, looking at the computer screen. "Three members. They vote on what happens to the forest. They decide if the logging can go forward."

<Dapsen Lumber Company,> Ax said. <That's what the Yeerks call this logging company. Very funny.>

"What's funny?" Marco asked.

<Dapsen. It's a Yeerkish word that means . . . well. Never mind what it means. It isn't polite.>

"Look at this document," Marco whispered. "'Preliminary permission to examine feasibility of . . . ' Hey. The Yeerks don't have final permission to begin logging. There's this commission that still has to decide. Three people. One has already said yes. Probably a Controller. One has voted definitely no. There's one guy left. Some guy named Farrand. Yikes!"

"What yikes?" Rachel asked.

"Yikes, as in he's coming for a visit to check the scene," Marco said. "End of the week. Then he'll vote. If that guy votes yes, the Yeerks are in business and we're in trouble."

"He'll vote yes," Rachel said darkly.

<I'm afraid that is true,> Ax agreed. <The Yeerks will make him a Controller.>

"Not if we stop them," Marco said.

"One thing at a time. We need to get out of here," Rachel said. "And we're not going back out the way we came in."

No one argued with that.

<I am making a slight change in the programming that may let me access this computer from Marco's home computer. And I can temporarily shut down the defenses from this computer,> Ax said. <But there are still guards outside. And Hork-Bajir in the next room.>

"Yeah. We'll have to move fast," Rachel said. "Cassie, can you morph? Can you morph the wolf? I'll stay right beside you the whole time."

Could I morph? The very idea made me sick. But even in my quaking fear I knew anything was better than going back down into that termite colony.

Five minutes later, Ax turned off the outer defenses, and we ran from that building.

I guess the Yeerks counted on their high-tech defenses too much. Without them, no one even shouted an alarm. By sheer, dumb luck we raced between the paths of two Controller guards.

No one yelled. No one fired a shot. We ran into the woods where Jake joined up with us.

No one said much on the way home.

CHAPTER 14

My parents expected me to be at Rachel's house. Her parents expected her to sleep over at my house. My house was easier to sneak into, so that's where we went.

It was almost dawn by the time we demorphed. We crept through my dark living room and up to my room, trying not to make the stairs squeak.

I loaned Rachel a big flannel shirt. She grabbed a blanket and a pillow and simply fell down on the floor beside my bed. I think she was asleep before she landed.

I crawled into my bed. My own, familiar bed. The sheets were cool. The comforter was *my* comforter. I belonged here. This was *my* place.

And yet nothing seemed familiar. The shadows cast by dim starlight on the walls . . . the shapes of shirts and overalls hung from big hooks on the walls . . . the bindings of books I'd read, right here in this room . . . none of it seemed real.

I closed my eyes, then opened them quickly.

How could it be? How could I remember what that chamber looked like, what the termite queen looked like when I'd had no eyes? But still, I remembered it all. I saw the chamber dug from the rotted wood by hundreds of workers. And I saw the huge queen.

I felt my pincers.

I hadn't just destroyed her. I had destroyed the entire colony. I had done it to save myself and my friends.

I wanted to throw up. But I would have had to get out of bed to run to the bathroom. And I felt like I never wanted to leave that bed again.

I love animals. I've been raised all my life around them. I love nature. But what did I really know about it?

I have *been* more animals than many people ever see in a lifetime. I have flown with the wings of an osprey. I've raced through the ocean in the body of a dolphin. I've seen the world through the eyes of an owl at night, and smelled the wind with all the keen senses of a wolf. I've flown upside down and backward in the body of a fly. Sometimes I go out into the far fields at night and become a horse and run through the grass.

And everything I've been, every animal, is either killer or killed.

In a million, million battles all around the world, on every continent, in every square inch of space, there was killing. From the great cats in Africa that cold-bloodedly search out the young and weak gazelles, to the terrible wars that are fought out in anthills and termite colonies.

All of nature was at war.

And, at the top of all that destruction, humans killed each other as well as other species, and now those same people have been enslaved and destroyed by the Yeerks.

Nature at its finest. Cute, cuddly animals who slaughtered to live. The color of nature wasn't green. It was red. Bloodred.

I realized tears were running down my cheeks and soaking my pillow. I would have cried out loud, but I didn't want Rachel to wake up. I would have screamed but my parents would have come running. And what could I have told them? Lies. More lies. Because in my world, I, too, was prey. The Yeerks were hunting me.

I was scared. I was alone. I didn't know what was going to happen to me.

And then I thought of the lost skunk kits. Unlovable little creatures, to most people. But they were scared and alone, too. If they were still alive.

CHAPTER 15

I guess I fell asleep eventually, because I dreamed. It wasn't a nightmare, though. It wasn't even about the termite world.

I was a mother. In my dream I was a mother, looking for her babies. I searched everywhere, even though I was hurt and in pain.

At last I found them. And, in my dream, they snuggled next to me.

When I woke up, the dream quickly evaporated. But it left behind a feeling of peace.

The sun was high in the sky. It was ten-fifteen in the morning. Late. Rachel had already showered and dressed.

"I can't believe you slept so well," Rachel

103

grumbled. "I had a seriously bad nightmare. Look, I gotta get home. Are you okay?"

"Sure," I said, rubbing the sleep from my eyes. "I mean . . . you know, last night and all . . . it wasn't like I was having some kind of breakdown or anything. It's just, you know. It creeped me out."

"Tell me about it," Rachel agreed. "But it's really no big deal if you think about it, Cassie. Termites get killed all the time. They were just termites. Bugs."

"Yeah."

She left. I don't know if she just had to get home, or if I made her uncomfortable. Rachel isn't usually a huggy kind of person. Having to treat me like a baby probably gave her the willies.

My mom was at work. My dad was off somewhere, I guess, because his truck was gone. I made some toast and drank some orange juice. Then I ate a piece of leftover veggie pizza.

I felt restless and weird. Like I was on the edge of something. Like life had gotten unbalanced since the day before.

"Rachel's right," I said out loud, just to hear a voice. "They're bugs. Termites. And besides, I got away in the end."

I walked outside to feel the sun on my skin. My human skin.

Without really thinking much about it, I went into the barn to the refrigerator we use to store perishable food for the animals. I took out a frozen grasshopper and stuck it in my pocket. And then I headed toward the edge of the forest.

<Hey, Cassie,> a thought-speak voice said as I crunched noisily through the woods. <What's going on?>

I looked up and saw Tobias go skimming by. He flared, turned on a dime, and landed on a branch. He dug his ripping talons into the soft bark.

"Not much," I said.

<I heard it was pretty bad last night.>

"Yeah? Who did you talk to?"

<Ax. Who else? He was definitely weirded out by the whole thing.>

I stopped walking. It was something in the way he said "weirded out." "Tobias, who else did you talk to?"

<Maybe Marco,> he said.

"And Marco told you I went nuts, right?"

<Actually, the word he used was "insane." Also "Looney Tunes." And "wacko." But he meant it all in the nicest possible way.>

I laughed bitterly. "Well, I guess I did go a bit wacko," I said.

<Welcome to the club,> Tobias said. <None

105

of us is going to come through all this completely normal. You know that. Too much fear.>

"Well, I'm pretty sick of it," I said. "I had to destroy the termite queen. I know, she was just a bug. But you know, who am I to decide that it's okay to kill one animal and not another? Here I am, the big Earth Mother, tree-hugger, animal-lover, as Marco would say, and when it gets down to it, I'm just like . . . "

<Just like me?> Tobias asked.

"Just like any predator," I said lamely.

<You feel bad because you had to kill the queen in order to survive.>

"I shouldn't have been there. It's *their* world, not mine. Those little tunnels in a rotten piece of wood — that's their whole universe. I invaded it. And when they got in my way, I reacted. Who does that remind you of?"

<Look, you are *not* a Yeerk, and termites are *not* human beings,> Tobias said. <There's no comparison.>

I didn't bother arguing. "Look, I have to morph. There's something I need to do."

<What?>

I sighed. "It's something stupid, all right? There's this mother skunk we have who's injured. She has a litter of kits who are going to die. I think I know where they are, more or less, but I can't get there walking like a human."

106

For a moment Tobias said nothing. <Skunk kits? Near the edge of the Yeerk logging compound?>

"Yes."

<I can show you where they are.>

For a frozen moment of time I refused to understand what he'd just said. I didn't want to think of why Tobias . . . why a red-tailed hawk would know the exact location of a litter of skunk babies.

I took a couple of deep breaths. I tried to keep my voice level. "Are they still alive?"

<There are four still alive,> Tobias said.

I felt an emotion I don't feel very often. I felt it boiling up inside me. I glared furiously at him. At the ripping talons. At the nastily curved beak.

I could picture the scene in my mind. The way he would have swooped down, raked those talons forward, snatched the defenseless kit off the ground and . . .

I was shaking. I laced my fingers together, just to stop them from trembling.

"I'm going to save what's *left* of them," I said. My voice didn't sound like my voice.

<I'll help you,> Tobias said.

CHAPTER 16

I used my osprey morph and flew behind Tobias as he led me directly to the spot I had seen the night before. I carried the frozen grasshopper in my talons. I didn't ask Tobias any questions, and he didn't say anything.

He pointed out the almost-invisible entrance to the skunks' lair. And then he flew away. I knew he'd go to Jake and tell him what I was doing. And I knew that I had hurt Tobias by treating him so coldly.

But, to tell you the truth, I didn't care right then. I just wanted to find those baby skunks. I don't know why, but somehow in my mind those baby skunks had become very important.

When Tobias was out of sight, I began to morph.

It wasn't a difficult morph. I kept eyes and ears and a mouth all the way through the change. Not like becoming a bug.

There was the now-familiar sensation of shrinking. And there was the surprise of having a huge, bushy tail growing from the base of my spine. But I had morphed a squirrel before. This was pretty close.

But the fur was a new experience. Oh, I'd grown fur before, but never any so long and luxurious and dramatic. This was a regular fur coat, so to speak. Mostly black, but with an impressive swipe of white down my back and into my tail.

The senses of the skunk were nothing dramatic. The hearing was a little better than human, maybe. The sense of smell was good. The sight not as good as my own human vision.

And the skunk's body was not swift or strong. I shuffled and sort of waddled when I tried to walk. When I tried to run I just ended up waddling a little more.

My front paws could grasp and hold things, but they were far inferior to my own human hands.

It was the skunk's mind and instincts that seemed strangest of all. I've been inside minds

109

that were all fear, or all hunger. Minds that were keyed up, like they lived on adrenaline.

But this mind, this package of instincts, was so . . . gentle. So unafraid. Not cocky and swaggering like a big cat, just unafraid.

I was an animal no bigger than a house cat. No sharp teeth or talons. And yet just about nothing in the forest messed with me. I felt the gentleness of absolute confidence.

I could hear the mewing sounds of the skunk kits within the burrow.

I waddled over to the opening and pushed my head inside. It was dark, but I could make out four of them. Tiny, helpless little things. No longer infants, but not yet able to defend themselves or hunt like skunks.

I know some people think animals don't have emotions. But those kits were happy to see me. And something in the mind of the skunk was relieved and joyful to see them.

I retrieved the frozen grasshopper, now completely thawed. I crawled inside that little hole in the dirt. I curled around, and the kits nuzzled up against me. I fed them the grasshopper.

I knew I only had two hours in morph. But even though I had just gotten up a few hours earlier, I suddenly felt sleepy. The meal was done. The kits wouldn't starve. And I was sleepy and very, very peaceful.

Even in my sleep I knew what was happening to me. See, I had always loved animals. Always. But now, I think was falling out of love.

Nature wasn't all cute and fuzzy. The strong ate the weak. The weak ate the weaker. It's what the Yeerks were doing: trying to make prey out of the ultimate predator, Homo sapiens.

WHUMP!

"Hey! Hey! Are you in there? Cassie!"

I woke up. Where was I? It was dark. Was I in my bedroom? Was I . . . oh, no, was I in the termite colony?!

The four kits still slept, curled up against me. I was in the skunks' den. <What?> I said.

"It's me, Jake. Cassie, get out of there. Now! You've been in morph for almost two hours!"

That woke me up all the way. I shot out of the burrow and instantly began to demorph.

Jake was standing there with Marco. Tobias was in the tree overhead.

I have seen Jake mad before. But I'd never seen him this mad. "What did you think you were doing?!" he yelled, without even waiting for me to become human. "You were ten minutes away from spending the rest of your life as a skunk!"

<I fell asleep,> I said. My mouth wasn't formed yet.

"Are you out of your mind? What is the matter with you?" I'd never noticed that Jake has this

111

vein that kind of pops out on his forehead when he's furious.

"Look, I'm sorry," I mumbled, as I finished demorphing.

He was a long way from forgiving me. "This is not why we have this ability. We are not trying to save every lost skunk in the world," Jake ranted. "We are an army. A small, weak, pathetic, out-numbered army. We have exactly six members. Tobias has already been trapped in morph. But he was trapped fighting the Yeerks. I can't believe you would nearly get yourself trapped in morph over some skunks!"

Marco stepped in and put a hand on Jake's shoulder and kind of pulled him back. "Look, it's okay, Jake. She's okay."

"Thanks to Tobias," Jake snapped. "No thanks to her."

I didn't know what to say. I was too shocked. And to be honest, I was pretty horrified by what I'd almost done.

"Marco. Tobias. Take a walk, okay?" Jake said. Then he turned and stood with his face just inches from mine. "I know you had a *real* bad experience last night. I've been there. I've had the nightmares. I know what's going on in your head right now."

"I'm fine," I muttered.

"Just shut up and listen to me," he said. But

the anger was gone now. "I care about you, Cassie. We all do. And we all need you."

"To win?" I said. "You need me to fight battles? What if I don't want to fight any more battles? What if I've had enough? I've done enough."

"You've done far more than enough. A hundred times more than enough. But the Yeerks are still here."

I shrugged. "The strong eat the weak," I said. "It's part of nature. Humans always win, other animals always lose. Maybe it's our turn to lose."

Jake nodded. "This isn't about some race called humans. It's about people we know. People we see every day. My brother, Tom, is one of *them*. So why don't you go tell Tom it's okay that he's a slave of the Yeerks because it's our turn to get hammered?"

He turned and walked away.

"Jake?"

He stopped.

"Jake? Um . . . my dad will have the skunk mother ready to be returned here in a day or so. I'm not going to just abandon these kits."

He put his hands on his hips and glared at me. "You can't stay in morph that long, and you know it."

"I know. But I have to make sure no predators come around. I have to get them food. And I have to morph at least some of the time, so they can

113

imprint on their mother here in the wild. Look . . . I know it seems stupid to you and Marco and probably everyone. But I have to do this."

<I'll watch them,> Tobias said.

I'd forgotten how good hawk hearing is.

"Tobias will keep watch. We'll work something out," Jake said. "We'll save the lousy skunks. After all, it's not like we have anything else to do. Aside from saving the world."

"Thanks, Jake," I said. "And . . . sorry. I didn't mean to scare you. I'll be okay now, I think."

He smiled his slow smile. "I'll be okay, too, Cassie. As long as you're around."

From a little ways off to our left I heard Marco make a loud gagging noise. It made me laugh. I must have been feeling better, to be able to laugh.

CHAPTER 17

"Well, this is more than slightly insane," Marco said. It was later that same day, Sunday evening. We were all gathered around the skunks' den. "We're going to raise little, stinky skunk babies?"

"What's so insane about that?" Rachel asked sharply. Good old Rachel. She thought it was ridiculous, too. But she's my best friend, and always backs me up.

"They're *skunks*," Marco said, looking from Rachel to Jake to Ax, like he was the only normal person in a mental ward.

"They're cute," Rachel said, glaring at Marco and generally looking like a girl who never used the word "cute."

115

"Ah. I see. 'Cute.' Well that certainly explains everything."

Jake cut in. "Cassie can't take them to the clinic or they may get used to humans. They're young. They'll imprint. So we are taking care of these . . . these skunks . . . until mommy skunk can come back from the hospital."

<Are skunks a sacred animal to humans?> Ax asked.

"*All* animals are sacred to Cassie," Marco said. "She's Doctor Doolittle and that animal guy who comes on *Letterman* all rolled into one."

<But you eat some animals,> Ax pointed out. <Cows, pigs, sheep, dogs.>

"We don't eat dogs!" I said.

<In some countries they do. I read it in the *World Almanac*.>

We had given Ax a *World Almanac* to help him learn about Earth. Ever since then, he'd become an expert on useless information. He could tell you the per capita income of Tanzania, or the long jump record at the Olympics.

"Well, we don't eat dogs in *this* country," Rachel said.

<Do you eat cats?>

"Um . . . excuse me?" Jake interrupted. He rubbed the bridge of his nose. He was obviously getting a headache. I could understand why. "Look, here's the deal: We are about three hundred yards from the edge of the Yeerk logging compound. They have sensors, they have guards. Tobias is up top keeping an eye out, so we're safe for now. But we can't get careless. Cassie, tell them what we want to do."

"Okay, while we're in school tomorrow and the next day, Ax and Tobias will protect the den. Ax will morph the mother skunk from time to time. Tobias will patrol from above. I'll bring Tobias frozen food so he doesn't have to hunt during that time."

"Oooh, Lean Cuisine Frozen Mouse entrees," Marco teased.

<I heard that,> Tobias said from somewhere up above the treetops.

"I know," Marco said, grinning smugly.

"Then, after school and through the night, the rest of us will work shifts. I'll do most of the skunk morphing, but in between times we'll have to have Jake and Rachel and Marco to help keep up a patrol."

Marco held up his hand.

"Yes, Marco?" I asked.

"Do we get some 'Save the Skunks' T-shirts and bumper stickers?"

"No one *has* to do this," I said. "Look . . . I know it seems stupid."

"Nah, it's not stupid," Marco said. "Let's see, I'm behind in my homework. My dad thinks I've joined a gang because I'm never around. I don't sleep much because every time I try I'm suddenly a termite again and I wake up screaming. I never get to just sit around and watch TV. And, in my *spare* time, I have to help figure out how we're going to keep the Yeerks from turning some guy named Farrand into a Controller so they can wipe out the forest and hunt down the Bird-boy and the universe's only almanac-reading Andalite. I mean, I knew the middle-school years would be tough, but this is a little much."

Jake gave Marco a long, skeptical look. "So, in other words, you'll be glad to help."

For once, it was Jake who made everyone laugh. Even Marco.

Marco shrugged. "You know, actually it's kind of a relief finding out Cassie is crazy. We *know* Rachel's nuts. We *know* I'm crazy. Cassie's been the only sane one for so long. Welcome to the loony bin, Cassie. Save the skunks! Hug the trees! Let dogs vote!"

The others all laughed. I laughed a little, too. Marco always made fun of my being an environmentalist. Usually it was okay, because I knew what I believed in.

But now his humor cut just a little deeper.

I wasn't saving the whales or the panda or the spotted owl. I was saving a handful of skunks.

There were plenty of skunks in the world. They weren't exactly endangered.

It all went back to the termite queen. A bug. I had killed a bug, and for some reason, that had shaken my deepest faith.

Maybe Marco was right. Maybe I was crazy.

CHAPTER 18

Over the next two days we protected and nurtured a foursome of baby skunks. And as impossible as it seems, it worked. More or less.

Maybe I'm kidding myself, but I think the others started enjoying it, too. Typically, it was Marco who decided, after his first shift guarding the skunks, that the kits needed names.

"Joey, Johnny, Marky, and C.J.," he announced, like it was obvious. "The Ramones. The godfathers of punk rock. They would be honored. The one with the white stripe that kind of goes really wide? That's Joey. Now, Johnny . . . "

At first, I was the only one to morph the skunk mother. Then Ax did it. Then the others, one by one. I almost felt jealous.

Right after school three days later, I went to the skunk burrow and found Tobias flying cover above the burrow.

<Hi, Cassie.>

"How's it going, Tobias?"

<Well, we had a little excitement. A hungry badger stopped by to check things out. But I chased him off.>

"So the kits are all right?"

<There are still four of them, if that's what you mean,> Tobias answered. <But they won't stay inside. They keep coming out and looking around. Especially Marky. This isn't good. Especially if they do it at night.>

I morphed into the skunk mother and crawled inside the den. Tobias was right — the kits were restless. They were growing fast, and they instinctively wanted to go out into the great big world beyond the burrow.

<I think I'm going to take them for a walk,> I told Tobias.

<Is that a good idea?>

<Sure. Why not? You should take a break. Stretch your wings.>

Tobias was relieved to have an excuse to take off. But as soon as he was gone I started to have doubts about my brilliant idea of taking the kits out for a stroll. How could I keep track of them? What if they wandered off?

121

But then, while I was debating, Marky made a wild dash outside and I had to scamper to catch up to him.

As soon as I appeared, though, the kit went meekly to stand behind me. One by one, the other three babies came out. And to my amazement, they lined up like obedient first-graders.

<Okay,> I said, although of course the kits couldn't understand me. <Let's take a walk.>

I waddled slowly away, took about ten steps, then turned to look back over my shoulder. The four of them were all lined up behind me. I was their mother, as far as they knew. And they were programmed to follow their mother.

I waddled off, feeling a little strange but happy.

We walked that way for half an hour. We paused to sniff things from time to time. Various animal scents, mostly.

And then, I realized something. We weren't supposed to just be going for a stroll. The kits were hungry. I was their mother. And it was my job to provide for them.

If I didn't teach them to catch bugs, they wouldn't survive. Skunks eat some plants, but they also eat crickets and mantises and grasshoppers and even shrews and mice.

I stopped walking and looked back at "my" kits. Four almost identical little balls of black-

and-white fuzz. Four curious little faces watching me. Waiting to see what I was doing. Eager to learn.

I'd been feeding them thawed frozen grasshoppers and thawed mice I'd brought from the clinic. Just as I'd been giving Tobias food since he was too busy to hunt properly. But these skunk kits couldn't be fed by humans all their lives.

Suddenly . . . a crashing sound! Something rushing through the woods, careless, wild, noisy. And coming right toward us!

I started to lead the kits back to the burrow, but the noise was getting closer. It was coming too quick! I tried to smell what it was, but the breeze was blowing the wrong way.

Then . . . ROWR! ROWR! ROWROWROWR!

A dog!

A wolf would have known better. A wolf would have seen the black-and-white fur and decided he had an appointment somewhere else. A bear would have known. Just about any wild animal knew better than to annoy an adult skunk.

But this big happy dog was not wild. He lived with humans. He knew absolutely nothing about skunks.

Without even thinking, I turned my back to the dog. I raised my tail in warning.

The dog kept coming. Drool was dribbling from one side of his mouth, and his tongue was hanging out the other side, and he was having about as good a time as a dog could have. He was in the woods, and he had a bunch of little black animals to play with.

The kits were still lined up. They were watching me intently. It almost made me want to laugh — if I could have. It was a big moment for them — they were about to learn why no sensible animal picked on adult skunks.

I had no experience in spraying. But the skunk mind within my own knew exactly what it was it had to do.

I aimed.

I looked over my shoulder to judge the distance.

I targeted that dog's face, and I fired.

Just at the instant when I fired, I had the strange sensation that I knew this dog from somewhere. But it was too late by then. Way too late.

At a distance of ten feet, the spray hit with the accuracy of a laser-guided smart missile.

ROWR? ROWR?

The dog stopped dead in his tracks. The look in his eyes was sheer horror. How could it be? How could the little black-and-white creature have done this to him?

And then, I heard something that made me feel really bad.

"Homer? What's the matter, boy?" Jake asked. "Oh. Ohhhhh, *Homer*! I told you not to follow me into the woods."

"Rrrreww rrrreeewww rrreeewww," Homer whined pitifully.

Jake, Marco, Rachel, and Ax all came up at a run. Marco was already laughing.

"You hosed Homer!" Marco giggled. "Cassie sprayed Homer! Wait, that *is* Cassie, right?"

I seriously considered pretending to be some other skunk.

<Sorry, Jake,> I said.

"Man, that is nasty," Rachel commented. "No offense, Cassie. But I mean . . . gag! Oh. Ugh."

<Fascinating,> Ax said. <That is possibly the worst thing I have ever smelled.>

Homer tried to nuzzle up to Jake, but as much as Jake loves his dog, he was not going for it. "I don't think so, big guy. I told you to stay home. But oh no, Homer, you had to come with me. Now, go home. HOME, boy!"

Homer decided home might be a better place than the forest, after all. He trotted off, tail between his legs.

<I believe the smell is causing me to become deranged,> Ax said calmly. <I may have to run away in panic.>

"Take me with you," Marco muttered.

125

"Well, this is perfect," Jake said. "Wonderful. My parents are going to so appreciate it when Homer gets back to the house reeking of skunk. Man, let's move away from this spot, okay? I mean, jeez, that's just awful."

We moved away from the scene of the stink, back toward the den. I led the kits inside, where they seemed happy to curl up and sleep. It had been an exciting outing for them.

I went back outside and demorphed. "Homer will be okay if you bathe him in tomato juice and leave him outside for a few days," I said to Jake. "Sorry."

"Not as sorry as Homer is," Jake said. "But we have bigger problems. Look, Cassie, we came to find you and Tobias. That guy Farrand? Ax and Marco tapped into the Yeerk computer at the logging camp."

"Yeah," Marco grinned. "The Ax-man knows his way around computers."

"Yeah, well, we found something out. Farrand isn't arriving this weekend. He's coming early. He's coming to cast the final vote on the logging in this forest. In fact, he'll be here in about an hour."

CHAPTER 19

"We have an hour to make plans and get ready," Jake said. "One hour. Less, since we have to get into position."

"Okay, what do we know?" Marco asked. "We know this Farrand guy is the one who makes the final decision on the Yeerks going forward. We know he's not a Controller or he would have already voted to let the logging begin."

"We know the Yeerks won't leave it to chance," Rachel said. "He's coming here to the site. They'll be ready to do an involuntary infestation. They have some slug sitting in a vat right now, waiting to crawl in the man's ear."

<They may just try to persuade this human,> Ax suggested. <They prefer voluntary infesta-

127

tions. And if they can get this human to give them his vote, they may simply let him go.>

"So what do we do, attack?" Rachel asked. "Just storm in and mess everything up?"

<Hey. Shhh,> Tobias said.

"What?" Rachel asked him.

<Don't you guys hear that? Even human ears should hear that.>

We all listened very intently. Then it came, carried on the breeze — the sound of diesel engines.

"Probably just our friends the Yeerks, moving their heavy equipment around. Putting it in nice, neat rows for the commissioner," Jake said. But then he thought it over and added, "Tobias? You mind going up to take a look?"

Tobias flapped his wings and soared above the treetops and out of sight.

"Okay, back to business," Jake said. "One way or the other, this Farrand guy is the key. If he votes yes, the Yeerks can log in this forest. If he votes no, they can't. Not without attracting way too much attention."

"Assuming they let Farrand live long enough to vote no," Rachel said.

"That's our job, then," I suggested. "We have to keep Farrand alive, and keep them from making him a Controller."

Everyone nodded.

"Too bad I have no idea how to do that," I admitted.

Just then, Tobias came rocketing down out of the sky. <They've already started!> he yelled as he shot past to land on a branch.

"Started what?" I asked.

<The Yeerks. They've started cutting trees. And they are coming this way!>

"Well," Jake said. "I guess that settles the question of whether the Yeerks are going to infest this guy."

"They don't care what this guy sees when he gets here," Rachel said. "They don't care about convincing him. This poor man already has a Yeerk slug with his name on it."

<You wouldn't believe how fast those machines can rip through trees!> Tobias said, obviously shaken up. <They're cutting trees like a farmer cuts wheat.>

<And we have one of your hours to help this commissioner,> Ax said. Then, he focused his two stalk eyes on the skunk burrow. <The small ones are right in the path of the loggers, if Tobias is correct.>

I expected Marco to make some snide remark about how no one cared about the skunks at a time like this. But to my amazement he said, "Hey, no one messes with the skunks. Those skunks are under official Animorph protection."

He winked at me and gave me a mocking clenched fist salute. "Save the skunks, Earth Sister!"

Marco is such a pain in the butt. But then, just when you think he's going to drive you crazy, he'll come through big time for you.

"Yeah, these are our skunks," Rachel said. "No one messes with our skunks."

"Excuse me? Hello?" Jake interrupted. "A plan? A plan, please?"

"Well . . ." I began.

"What?" Jake asked me.

I shrugged. "If Farrand is the key, we need to grab the key. Right? Chances are they'll have to turn the force field off in order to get him into the camp. That's when we get him away from the Yeerks. No matter what it takes."

"Grab Farrand," Marco said. "Simple. Elegant. And yet, given the Yeerk power in that compound of theirs, completely suicidal. I'm surprised at you, Cassie. Usually Rachel's the one to come up with a totally suicidal plan."

"You have a better idea?" Jake asked Marco.

"We could go home and watch TV."

"I'll take that as a no." Jake rubbed his hands together. "Okay, then. We snatch this Farrand guy as soon as he shows up. In the meantime, we have to slow down those tree-cutting machines."

Rachel grinned. "Cool."

I felt sick.

CHAPTER 20

There was only one way for a person to reach the Yeerk logging camp by car. They had to drive down the long, dirt road that the Yeerks had cut through the forest.

Jake wanted me to go with Tobias and see if we could spot Farrand coming in.

Jake made some quick decisions. He, Marco, Rachel, and Ax took off, leaving me with Tobias.

I looked up ruefully at Tobias. "You and me, I guess."

<I'm always glad to have you along,> Tobias said.

I began to morph into an osprey. It was my bird of prey morph, and the only thing I had that could keep up with Tobias in the air.

"Look, Tobias? This has been bothering me. And since . . . you know . . . I want to get this off my chest. I'm sorry I got mad at you over the skunk kit. You were just doing what you had to do," I said.

I could feel my bones thinning and hollowing out. Gray feathers began to paint their patterns on my arms.

<I could live off food you guys brought me,> Tobias said. <I don't *have* to hunt.>

"Okay, then why do you?" I asked, just before my mouth mutated into a beak.

<Because I'm not just a human. I'm also a hawk. Hawks hunt live prey. Would it be better if I let you do my killing for me? Is it more moral if I eat a frozen mouse you get from some supplier?>

<Look, Tobias, I know all about how nature works. I know about predators and prey. It's just . . . it's just confusing. I mean, where does right and wrong come into it?>

Snowy-white feathers were growing all down my front, replacing the fabric of my morphing suit. My feet were becoming pale gray talons.

<I don't know. I guess if I were running around killing animals I didn't intend to eat, that would be wrong. But hawks have a right to live, just as much as a mouse or a skunk.>

My human eyes were giving way to the incredibly amazing hawk vision. There was some color distortion because these eyes were adapted for seeing through water. The osprey eats fish. Nature designed them to see fish, even below the shimmering surface of a lake or river.

<Ready to fly?> Tobias asked.

I flapped my wings a couple of times. <Let's go,> I said, trying to sound like Rachel.

Tobias flapped his wings, caught a headwind, and suddenly shot almost straight up. I opened my wings and contracted the tireless flying muscles. Flap, flap, flap, and I also caught the breeze. I flapped to get above the trees, then a stronger breeze came up and I soared high.

It's like stepping on a very fast escalator. Zoom! I flapped hard, wanting the sensation of speed.

Tobias was ahead of me, and as I flew, I watched him. I watched the incredibly subtle movements of his wings. He almost seemed to be able to move individual feathers. For him, the wind was not invisible. It was a road, as clear as if it was blacktop.

As I followed him, I sensed the osprey brain beneath my own, adjusting and reacting to the wind. My eyes saw every small detail. They marked each animal, each hole where an animal might be hiding. I saw a bright stream, and saw the shadows of fish flitting through the rocks.

My osprey had been designed by nature for

this: flying high and finding prey. Just like Tobias.

We flew up and up. The tops of trees were like some bumpy lawn beneath us. I could see all of the Yeerk logging camp. And I could see the massive yellow machines that were slicing through the trees like hot knives through butter. Already there was an ugly scar of stumps. A scar that spread like some terrible disease, eating the forest away.

Tobias veered right, toward the long, winding road through the trees. I banked my wings and went after him.

The stream joined a small river, rushing and bubbling alongside the road. Through the water, through the foam and bubbles, I saw the schools of fish darting. And I could feel the osprey's brain considering the situation. Measuring the distances. Calculating the angles. Planning the way it would skim low over the surface of the water, then lower its ripping talons at just the perfect moment to strike. To snatch a fish right out of the water.

I knew that Tobias was making the same calculations as he flew over mice and rats and rabbits . . . and skunks.

Tobias and I were two superb, beautiful killers, riding the wind, while our prey cowered beneath us.

But he was right. We had as much of a right to live as any of our prey. And we had been designed by millions of years of evolution to be predators.

<There,> Tobias said. <A Jeep.>

I looked and saw the vehicle coming down the road. Then, with my amazingly acute hawk vision, I saw right through the windows, as though the glass were the surface of a stream. <Three guys. One driving, and one beside him. There's one guy in the backseat, and he looks older.>

<Yep. And on the side of the Jeep it says Dapsen Lumber. My guess is the driver and the other guy are Controllers. The guy in the backseat is looking all around like he's very interested in what's going on.>

<They'll reach the camp in a few minutes. As soon as we see how this Farrand guy reacts, we'll know if he's already been made into a Controller,> I said.

<How's that?>

<The Yeerks have gone ahead with logging,> I explained. <If Farrand is still a true human, he'll be massively upset. If he's calm, he's already one of them.>

<Good point,> Tobias said.

<What do we do? I mean, if he's a Controller already?> I asked.

135

<I don't know. I guess we focus on attacking the logging operation itself.>

<Really? You know what we'd do if he were a nonhuman Controller?> I asked. <We'd go after him and whatever happened, happened. Right?>

<You mean, like a termite?> Tobias asked dryly.

<Yeah. That's exactly what I mean,> I said.

<Look, Cassie, you're human. Homo sapien. Your job is to keep yourself and your species alive. That's all nature wants from you. That's the whole point of evolution — to survive.> He sounded angry.

We were following the Jeep now, heading back toward the logging camp. It would happen in just a few minutes. In just a few minutes Farrand would see what was going on, and we would know what he truly was.

One of us, or one of *them*.

<Survive,> I said flatly.

<That's the law of nature. The number one law. And humans are part of nature.>

<Then so are the Yeerks, and we're no better than them.>

<I guess we'll have to worry about that one later,> Tobias said. <Look.>

The Jeep pulled to a stop in front of the Yeerk fortress.

Farrand flung open his door and jumped out. I

could easily see him waving his arms. Even from where I was I could see the anger on his face.

Then from the building there came a man.

And yet . . . this man felt wrong. Even from up in the air, I felt a chill that seemed to emanate from him.

<*Him,*> Tobias said.

I knew instantly what Tobias meant.

<I only saw him once in a human morph, but it's him,> Tobias said.

Visser Three.

CHAPTER 21

Visser Three.

The leader of the Yeerk invasion of Earth. The only Yeerk in all the universe to have taken control of an Andalite body. The only Yeerk in all the universe with the power to morph.

It shouldn't have surprised me that he would use his human morph. It made sense.

And yet I felt a cold rage deep inside me at the sight. It wasn't logical, but I felt it just the same. He was a fake human. He was using human DNA and human form as part of his plan to enslave all of humanity.

<Visser Three,> I said to Tobias.

<Yeah,> he agreed. <He looks so normal. Except for the fact that he gives you the creeps.>

<I have a bad feeling about this,> I said. <I don't think they're going to wait long. I think they're going to take Farrand right away.>

Farrand was walking toward Visser Three, still waving his hands wildly toward the heavy machinery that was chewing through the trees. Visser Three was smiling. It was not a nice smile.

<Where are Jake and the others?> Tobias wondered.

<Oh, man,> I said. <This is going to happen real — >

All of a sudden, Visser Three lashed out and slapped Farrand across the face. The commissioner staggered back. He held a hand to his cheek.

The two men from the Jeep rushed to grab Farrand's arms. Farrand was an older man. He was helpless.

<Cassie. Look. That's either Jake, or there is some other tiger loose in these woods!>

I looked toward the clearing. Now I could see it — a huge, orange-striped tiger was racing toward Farrand. But he was too far away. It had all happened too suddenly. Jake wasn't in position. I didn't even know where the others were. Probably still morphing.

<It's up to us,> I said.

I adjusted my wings, aimed for Visser Three, and dove. Down, down, down. Faster and faster, till my wings were vibrating and my bones were rattling from the speed.

The target, Visser Three's human head, grew larger. Larger. Larger!

I raked my talons forward, I flared my wings just enough to keep from overshooting, and I struck. I could feel my talons bite into his scalp. And then I was out of there, carried away by my own momentum.

"Aaarrrgghh!" the Visser yelled.

At the same instant, Tobias hit one of the guys from the Jeep. Tobias has more experience than I do. His aim is better. The guy he hit would be wearing an eyepatch for the rest of his life.

<Yeee hah!> Tobias cried.

Farrand broke free of his remaining captor and ran.

"Get him!" Visser Three yelled. "Full alert!"

The uninjured guard went after Farrand. He caught him easily and knocked him facedown in the dirt. I saw Jake closing in fast, a black-and-orange streak.

Looking past him, I saw that there was a second battle out by the edge of the forest. Two wolves — Rachel and Marco — were on the Controllers operating the machines. The perimeter guards had come running, automatic weapons ready.

Suddenly, fast as a gazelle, Ax ran to help

Rachel. The nearest guard turned to take a shot. Ax's tail flashed, and the Controller no longer had a way to pull a trigger.

Just beneath me, the other Controller from the Jeep kicked Farrand, who was struggling to get up. That was too much for me. I wheeled in the air and went back for a second run.

<Cassie!> Tobias cried a warning.

The front door of the building flew open and they began spilling out — a half dozen human-Controllers, each armed. And worse . . . far worse, four big Hork-Bajir.

But it was too late to back off. I was already diving.

BLAM! BLAM! BLAM!

I heard the first two bullets go whizzing past me.

I felt the third bullet hit my wing. It went straight through my right wing, and I tumbled from the air, suddenly as ungainly as a chicken.

I fell. Helpless, I fell.

WHUMP!

I slammed hard into the ground.

Dizzy and confused, I thought I saw Jake leap toward a Hork-Bajir warrior. But I couldn't be sure. I was fading. Fading . . .

My world grew small and dark. I could no longer see anything far away. I could focus only on the ground right before me.

An ant was marching by, carrying a dead bug. Maybe I was just imagining things, as I sank into unconsciousness. Maybe my brain was making up things that weren't there. But I could almost have sworn that the ant was carrying the dead, dried-out husk of the termite queen.

And then everything went black.

CHAPTER 22

I woke up in a sort of large box. It was dark, but not totally without light. There were small round holes drilled in the sides of the box. Airholes. I could see the commissioner, Farrand, unconscious on the floor beside me.

He looked old. He was mostly bald and had hair growing out of his ears. There was blood trickling from a shallow cut on his forehead.

"Turn on the perimeter defenses!" Visser Three yelled.

I could hear him clearly. I was still an osprey, but ospreys have good hearing. It was strange, being able to hear the Yeerk Visser's voice. We always encountered him when he was in his own

143

stolen Andalite body. Then he communicated only in thought-speak.

"You! And you! Keep your eyes on that box," Visser Three snapped. "If anything . . . *anything*, no matter how small tries to get out of there, destroy it! There's an Andalite bandit in that box, and there had better be an Andalite bandit in that box when this is over. Or I'll destroy you both!"

Andalite bandit. That was me. Of course, if I didn't get out of the box, I would have to demorph eventually and Visser Three would see the truth — that I was a human.

And I would have to demorph soon. My wing felt like it was on fire. The pain was terrible.

"Visser! The Andalite bandits have turned the heavy equipment toward us!" someone yelled.

"Then turn on the force field!"

"But . . . but Visser . . . our own people will be trapped outside of the force field."

The Visser's voice suddenly became very quiet. A very dangerous kind of quiet. "Did I just hear you question my order?"

"No! No Visser! I'm turning on the force field!"

Farrand moaned. He moved his head a little, but then became quiet again.

Okay, Cassie, think. Think!

Obviously, my friends were still fighting. They

must be winning, or the Visser would not turn on the force field.

They had seized control of some of the machines and turned them against this building. As soon as the force field went up, the heavy equipment would be useless.

And time was on the side of the Yeerks. Visser Three would have called in more help. The Bug fighters full of fresh Hork-Bajir could be landing any minute. When that happened, all would be lost.

We were done for.

No! Think, Cassie! This was the game of predator and prey. This was war. What was the Yeerks' weakness? What did they need that I could take away?

Farrand moaned again.

Of course!

I took a deep breath. I began to morph quickly out of the pain-wracked osprey body, back to my own human form. Morphing works on DNA, and DNA is not affected by injuries. My reconstructed human body would be normal.

It was cramped in the box, with two humans in there. I was hunched over Farrand when his eyes fluttered open. I was already beginning my next morph. What the man saw was the face of a girl. But a face that was sprouting luxuriant black-and-white fur.

His eyes closed again. He would think it was all a dream. Hopefully.

"Hah!" I heard Visser Three crow. "The force field has stopped them!"

"Visser! The first Bug fighters will land here in fifteen minutes."

<Got them!> Visser Three said. <This time, I've got them!>

He was using thought-speak. The Visser had demorphed.

I focused all my thoughts. I knew what I had to do. But it was dangerous. I had to communicate with the Visser in thought-speak. And I had to do it without giving him any hint that I was a human.

No long conversation. Monotone voice. As few words as possible. No images of any kind.

<Visser,> I said. <I'll kill the human.>

That was Visser Three's weakness — he needed Farrand alive. That was the pressure point. By threatening to kill Farrand, I threatened the Visser's plan.

See, you can't make a Controller out of a corpse.

The Visser instantly understood.

<Everyone in this room! Weapons on the box! Be prepared on my command to shoot the Andalite without hitting the human! It may be in

any sort of wild, deadly animal morph! Do not let it escape.>

I got into position. The human me was scared. But the skunk me was perfectly calm. The skunk knew it had the ultimate weapon.

Suddenly, the door of the box flew open.

Visser Three stood there in his Andalite body, with his deadly Andalite tail cocked and ready to strike.

Beside him, on either side, stood half a dozen armed human-Controllers. And in between the humans, towering above them, five huge Hork-Bajir warriors.

The human-Controllers leveled their weapons.

The Hork-Bajir had weapons, too, but they didn't need them. Hork-Bajir *are* weapons, seven feet of ankle blades, knee blades, elbow blades, forehead spikes, and armored tail — like Stegosaurus meets Klingon.

All this awesome deadly destructive power stared down at me.

Visser Three aimed his Andalite stalk eyes at me. His main eyes were already staring in amusement.

<This is the best you could do, Andalite scum?> He laughed. <Such a terrifying beast you've morphed!> He laughed again.

He laughed at the chubby, cat-sized black-

and-white animal in the box. Laughed at the way I stood with my back to him, tail raised, looking over my shoulder.

A skunk can fire its scent with amazing accuracy up to about fourteen feet.

The Visser was only six feet away.

<Kill it,> Visser Three ordered coldly.

But I fired first.

A skunk can fire its scent in five to seven shots.

I fired once and hit the Visser in the face.

I fired again and hit the nearest Hork-Bajir on the left. Again and hit two human-Controllers. Again and again, all within about three seconds.

<Aaaarggghh!>

"Oh, guh, guh, ohhhhh. Ohhhh!"

"*Herunt gahal!* Stink! Arrrr!"

The Visser staggered back, blinded and reeling from the mighty stench. The human-Controllers covered their mouths with their hands. Some even dropped their weapons.

The Hork-Bajir I was worried about. I didn't know if Hork-Bajir even had a sense of smell.

Turns out they do.

Turns out they have an excellent sense of smell. Too bad.

The Hork-Bajir were the first to panic. One fired his Dracon beam wildly.

<Don't shoot, you fools!> Visser Three screamed. <You'll hit the human! Or me!>

Actually, what they had hit was the floor. A big, smoldering hole appeared in the wood.

"Reeking *fernall gahal*!" one Hork-Bajir kept bellowing in the odd mix of English and their own tongue.

Then the Hork-Bajir lost it completely. They turned and ran for the door.

Personally, I didn't see what they were so excited about.

It didn't smell bad to me.

CHAPTER 23

They ran. The human-Controllers, the Hork-Bajir, and Visser Three. They ran from the horror of my skunk smell.

I waddled as far as the doorway.

I saw an amazing scene. The force field was still on. Three massive tree-cutters, diesel engines roaring and billowing smoke, were straining against the force field like mad dogs on a leash.

Inside the force field, the totally demoralized Yeerk forces.

Outside the force field, a bizarre zoo — a tiger, a grizzly bear, a gorilla. And something no human zoo had ever held — an Andalite.

Jake, Rachel, Marco, and Ax.

Around the clearing, a handful of human-

Controllers and Hork-Bajir warriors sat nursing wounds. Some were just lying in the dirt.

It was a weird and tense scene. If the force field came down, the tractors and tree-cutters would hit the building within seconds.

On the other hand, even though they were reeking of skunk smell, and staggering and half-blind, the forces inside the field were stronger than Jake, Rachel, Marco, and Ax.

Of course, if the tree-cutters hit the building, they would probably kill Farrand. The Yeerks didn't want that. Neither did we, but Visser Three didn't know that.

<What happened?> Jake asked me in a private thought-speak whisper.

<I sprayed them,> I said. <They didn't like it.>

I'm pretty sure tigers can't normally smile. But I could have sworn Jake did.

Jake must have privately told Ax what happened. Ax was the only one we could trust to speak to Visser Three. He was the only true Andalite.

<Visser,> Ax said. <It seems to me that we have a standoff.>

<Don't try to bargain with me, fool,> Visser Three sneered. <I have forces on the way.>

Ax nodded. <I wonder how your Blade ship will smell after you spread your newly acquired stench through it?>

151

<The smell . . . it will go away,> the Visser said.

"Visser, my human host has a memory of —" one of the human-Controllers began to say.

The Visser's tail blade snapped through the air. It pressed against the human-Controller's throat. A twitch would send the Controller's head flying.

<Do not interrupt me,> the Visser said calmly. <You were saying?> he asked Ax.

<The smell would go away in about seven Earth days . . . if you were in the open air,> Ax said calmly. <In a spacecraft? Airtight, closed up, cramped? You'll never lose the smell. Ever. However . . . thanks to Andalite chemical technology there is a way to remove the stench. Let the human Farrand go free. He's unconscious and hasn't seen what you are. Let him go, we'll give you the secret of neutralizing the stench, and we all walk away.>

<I'll dispose of you myself!> the Visser shrieked. <Andalite filth!>

<Visser, we both know how impossible it is to remove a smell once it gets into a spacecraft. You would need a full refitting at a major space dock. Your Blade ship would be intolerable.>

Visser Three just stood there. Just stood there and stared. His stalk eyes drooped a little.

<Get the human,> he muttered to his Hork-Bajir.

"Visser . . . " one Hork-Bajir moaned, clearly reluctant to go back where the smell was even stronger.

<This has not been a good day for me,> Visser Three said. <Would you really like to feel as bad as I do?>

The two Hork-Bajir went back inside and very quickly reappeared, dragging Farrand. They dropped him in the dirt.

<Have one of your men drive him to the nearest human hospital. When he is safe, we will tell you the secret. And no tricks. We'll be watching.> Ax rolled his stalk eyes skyward. Visser Three followed the direction of his gaze, and saw, high in the sky, a bird of prey with a rust-red tail.

<You do realize that one day I will have you all,> Visser Three said. <With all your clever tricks, I will still find you.>

<No, I do not think so,> Ax said. <We are sure to smell you coming.>

CHAPTER 24

The Yeerks drove Farrand to the hospital. Once we knew he was safe, Ax told Visser Three how a certain kind of juice would help get rid of the skunk smell.

The Visser was still screaming when we disappeared into the woods.

The next day, Jake, Marco, Rachel, Ax, and I were able to bring the skunk mother back to her den. She waddled inside, and a few minutes later, waddled back out followed by Joey, Johnnie, Marky, and C.J.

They ignored the four humans and the Andalite completely. After all, mother skunk was back with her kits. And mother skunk wasn't afraid of anything.

"They grow up so fast," Rachel said, as they shuffled and snuffled and waddled past us in single file.

"I guess the real mother skunk will give them different names," Marco said. He was joking. I think.

"Well, anyway, the forest is safe for baby skunks now," Jake said.

Jake had morphed a housefly to spy on Farrand in the hospital. The commissioner was fine. The first thing he did when he regained full consciousness was make a phone call to say that he was voting against logging in the forest.

In fact, according to Jake, Farrand swore he'd never, ever even listen to another word from Dapsen Lumber. And there was a good chance he'd press charges.

It also seemed, according to Farrand, that even the animals of the forest had risen up against the loggers. He claimed that he himself had been visited by the spirit of a giant skunk with the eyes of a human girl.

"Have a good life, little skunks," Marco said to the skunk family. Tiny, furry little masters of the forest.

Everyone was smiling and looking pretty pleased with themselves. But I was still confused.

As we walked toward home back through the

155

forest, Jake hung back with me, letting the others move ahead.

"You don't seem all that happy," Jake said. "You miss being a skunk mommy?"

I smiled. "No. I mean, yes, a little. But that's not it."

"So? So what's bothering you?"

I shrugged. "Nothing makes sense to me. Tobias eats one of the skunk kits, then he helps save the rest. I kill the termite queen to save myself and my friends, then I feel bad about it. But when it came down to it again, I went after Visser Three without hesitation. One minute I was a rat being chased by guys with sticks, the next minute I'm bringing dead mice to Tobias, who's guarding skunks he would normally have tried to eat. Somehow it's part of the same big system. How does it all make sense?"

Jake looked like he was sorry he started the conversation. "Um . . . boy, Cassie, I don't know."

"Okay, just tell me this. Am I a part of nature, so I should just live by the laws of nature, kill to eat, kill or be killed? Or am I something different because I'm a human?"

We walked in silence while Jake thought it over. I felt sorry for him. I know he'd rather have been discussing Spiderman versus Batman with Marco.

"Well, I guess you're both," Jake said at last.

"I mean, you are the person who got rid of the termite queen. You're also the person who went out of her way to save a bunch of skunks. Just like Tobias ate a skunk kit one day, then saved them the next."

"That's not much help," I said. "That just means humans are kind of in-between — still partly wild animals, doing whatever it takes to survive, and partly . . . partly I don't know what. Maybe something more than the other animals."

"Well, I know one thing. All the animals take care of themselves. But only one animal has the intelligence and the power to help save all the other species."

I nodded. "You're pretty smart sometimes, Jake," I said.

"Just sometimes?"

"You're right. Only one animal can help to save all the other animals. Only humans can do that. Of course, we have to save ourselves first." I sighed. "It's still too complicated."

I saw a shadow flash overhead. I looked up and saw Tobias. He dropped down into the trees and reappeared on a branch just up the trail.

"Hi, Tobias," I called up to him.

<Hi, Cassie. Hello everyone. Hello, hello, hello.>

He was definitely feeling pretty smug about something.

157

"What's up, Bird-boy?" Marco asked him.

<I've just been checking on our friends at the logging camp. They now have two entire truckloads of juice. They've made trip after trip for juice. They dug out a big pit in the ground and made a kind of swimming pool filled with the stuff. Visser Three's been in it most of the night and all this morning. Judging by the way everyone is staying back, I'm guessing he still stinks. Plus,> Tobias added with a slightly evil laugh, <the Visser is now a very lovely, attractive shade of purple.>

"Gee, that's too bad," Rachel said. "I feel so sorry for him."

<Soon he may begin to suspect the truth,> Ax said.

"Think maybe we should have told him the truth? That it's *tomato* juice, not *grape* juice that washes away skunk smell?" I asked.

We all looked at each other, and broke up laughing at the same moment.

"Nah, I didn't think so," I said.

<Marco. What are you doing?>

It was Ax. I scampered down off the beetle, feeling like I'd been caught doing something wrong. The beetle ran on, relieved to have escaped. If beetles can feel relief.

<Nothing. I was just letting the spider be a spider.> It was a pretty good answer, I thought. <I guess its instincts kind of carried me away.>

<Marco, I morphed the identical spider,> Ax said.

I felt a wave of guilt and shame suddenly swell up inside me. <Ax, it was just a cockroach. Who cares? Come on, we have a job to do.>

<Sometimes humans worry me,> Ax said. . . . <I think it's this way.> He took the lead and I saw him moving in front of me, a big spider scurrying effortlessly on his eight legs.

I fell in behind him. I was calm now. The incredible, insane rush of the chase was over. Now the spider was just a tool I was using.

Suddenly, from the sky . . . something fell toward me!

It landed right between Ax and me. A grasshopper, three, four times our size. It looked like an elephant.

Then . . . THWAP! It fired its huge hind legs and shot into the air. It disappeared as quickly as it had arrived.

We raced on through the forest, covering the two hundred feet between us and the edge of the party. I sensed the nearness of humans. I "heard" vibrations that might have been speech, but the voices were too garbled to make any sense out of.

<Hey, Marco, Ax, you guys around?>

It was Jake's thought-speak voice.

<Yes, Prince Jake,> Ax answered. <We are here.>

<We're not pretty, but we're here,> I added.

<Cool. I'm not exactly handsome myself. I'm a fly morph. Haven't found our boy Erek yet, though.>

Something massive and slow appeared in the air above me. I scampered sideways. It landed slowly with a loud WHOOOMPHHH!

A human foot. A shoe. Nike.

<You know, I'd been worrying someone might step on me,> I said. <But humans are so slow.>

<Be careful anyway,> Jake said. <Let me know if you find Erek.>

<I don't know how I'm supposed to recognize him,> I complained. <These spider eyes aren't good at seeing distances. And human heads seem to be way up in the clouds, from where I'm crawling down here.>

But Ax and I went on, skittering swiftly through a forest of huge, slow-moving legs and feet.

Then, right in front of me, I saw it.

It looked like a bare human foot. Except that I could see through the skin. Through the toenails. With my eight strange, distorted spider eyes I could see right through the electronic haze of the hologram.

I could see what was beneath the hologram.

I saw what looked like interlocking plates of steel and ivory. The "foot" had no toes. In fact, it wasn't shaped like a human foot. More like a paw.

It was not human. And everything in my tingling, buzzing, hyper spider's senses told me it was not alive.

<Ax?>

<Yes, I see it.>

<What is it?>

<I do not know.>

<It looks like a machine, almost. Like it's made out of metal.>

<Yes,> Ax said. <I think your old friend Erek may be an android.>

First came the Yeerks.
Now, prepare for something even stranger....

ANIMORPHS

It all happened in a flash. Erek ran. He tripped.
He sprawled forward, out into the street. WHAM!
He slammed into the broad side of a passing bus.

And then...for just a second, Erek wasn't there
anymore. Something else was there where he had
been. Something that seemed to be made of
patches of steel and milk-white plastic.

Then, in the next split second, Erek was back.
A normal boy, lying winded on the sidewalk.

<What was that,> Tobias asked.

<It wasn't human,> I said.

<Yes,> Ax said. <I think your friend Erek may be
an android.>

ANIMORPHS #10:
THE ANDROID

K.A. Applegate

**COMING
IN AUGUST**